CALCULATE

Calculated Risk

a novel by
Dougal Haston

Foreword by Doug Scott

with an additional note for 2006
by Robin N.Campbell

BÂTON WICKS · LONDON
2006

First published in 1979 by Diadem Books
reprinted in 1980

This edition published by Bâton Wicks in 2006
ISBN 1-898573 66 2

All trade enquiries to
Cordee, 3a DeMontfort Street
Leicester LE1 7HD

Printed in Singapore
by the Kyodo Printing Company

CONTENTS

DOUGAL HASTON'S CLIMBS

Among UK rock and ice climbs, Alpine climbs and Himalayan /Greater Range ascents the following stand out – (w) indicating winter ascent:

BEN NEVIS 1957-1959: Staircase Climb (w)(Jimmy Stenhouse), Minus Two Gully (w) (Jimmy Marshall and Stenhouse), The Bat (Robin Smith).

GLEN COE / GLEN ETIVE 1958-1965: Dingle, Swansong, Lechers, Meander, The Prowl, The Kneepad, Dick Smersh, Gearr Aonach Gully A Central Branch (w), Aonach Dubh North Ridge – South Wall, Aonach Dubh Girdle, Turnspit, Hee Haw, Kuf, Drainpipe Corner (w), Stook, Frustration, Bo Weevil, The Big Ride, Cut the Grass, Attilla, Aryan, Greez. On these he was partnered, variously, by Jim Brumfit, Robin Campbell, Joy Heron, Jimmy Marshall, Bugs McKeith, Elly Moriarty, M. Sclater, T. Shearer, Robin Smith, Jimmy Stenhouse, Brian Wakefield, Andy Wightman and Graham Tiso.

CREAGH DUBH, NEWTONMORE: 1964-1966 Inbred, Mount, Cuckold, Gham, Prack, Epar, Romp, Erse, Hayripi, Great Wall Girdle (all first ascents with, variously, T. Gooding, Moriaty, Arthur Ewing, R.K. Holt, Heron, Mike Galbraith and Campbell)

OLD MAN OF HOY 1966 South-East Arête (first ascent with Pete Crew)

THE ALPS: 1963 Eiger North Face (Rusty Baillie); 1966 Eiger Direct (first ascent with Jörg Lehner, Gunther Ströbel, Roland Votteler, Sigi Hupfauer); 1972 Aiguille du Argentiere (new route left of the Messner route with Chick Scott); Aiguille du Midi, North-West Couloir (first winter ascent with Guy Neithardt); 1974 Mönch North Face Left Flank (first ascent, in winter, with Guy Neithardt); 1975 Aiguille du Triolet, North Face Direct (first winter ascent with Chris Bonington); 1976 North-West Couloir of the Mönch (Ole Eistrup)

PATAGONIA: 1968/69 Cerro Torre (attempt on the South-East Ridge with Peter Crew, Martin Boysen, Mick Burke and José Luis Fonrouge).

NEPAL / INDIA HIMALAYA: 1970 Annapurna South Face (first ascent with Don Whillans, with an Anglo-American team led by Chris Bonington); 1971 / 1972 Everest South-West Face attempts when, on both, he reached the end of the upper right hand snow ramp; 1974 Changabang (first ascent of peak with Doug Scott, Martin Boysen, Chris Bonington, Balwant Sandhu and Tashi Sherpa; 1975 Everest South-West Face (first ascent with Doug Scott, with a British team led by Chris Bonington).

ALASKA: 1977 Mount McKinley or Denali (first alpine-style ascent of the South Face with Doug Scott).

FOREWORD

On January 17, 1977 Dougal Haston was overwhelmed and
killed by an avalanche while ski-ing the Riondaz, a minor
peak above the Swiss ski resort of Leysin. A few days earlier
Dougal had finished penning this semi-autobiographical novel.
An exact typed copy of Dougal's original writing was completed a few weeks later by Ariane Giobellina. Although
Dougal would clearly have done further work on the manuscript had he lived, it was felt by some of his friends that this
first version should be published as it contained such a wealth
of information about this internationally known mountaineer
that did not appear in his autobiography *In High Places*.

Very little of the original manuscript has been altered,
though it has been tightened and sub-edited by Lucy Rees on
behalf of the publishers. It is quite likely that on a second
manuscript Dougal might have moderated certain passages
and given greater breadth to the characters. Nevertheless it is
refreshing to read a book like this, free from discretion of
secondary considerations. With this in mind the reader might
better understand the bold assertions and opinions that appear
in the book, particularly in relation to women. In his novel
Dougal depicts a way of life that may not be to everyone's
taste—nevertheless the code of this particular road is well-
defined and rigorous. Because he had an ability to transcend
certain conventions, Dougal became the centre of every
circle in which he found himself.

The irony of the ski-ing incident described in the book
when Jack McDonald races a powder snow avalanche on La
Riondaz, and escapes death by skill and anticipation, is
matched against the incident in real life in which Dougal
perished. On January 17 the warnings were up not to ski
above Leysin, but Dougal had not taken the risks lightly as
the continental press suggested at the time. To ski down La

Riondaz in those conditions was something he had long planned to do. He was obviously aware of the dangers as the book confirms.

At whatever level the reader delves into this book he will find both a good adventure story but also an undercurrent of explanation of the wealth of human situations and relationships that can accompany the practice of extreme risk-taking.

DOUG SCOTT
August, 1979

A Note on Mountain Fiction *by Robin N. Campbell*

As Audrey Salkeld and Rosie Smith have pointed out, there is a good deal of mountaineering fiction, some of it good, and some written by well-known mountaineers.[1] It is not too hard to come up with well-known mountaineers who have written bad fiction. Bill Murray produced four romantic thrillers, which do not thrill and whose characters would make a dead eunuch seem frisky, and Wilfrid Noyce wrote a novel, *The Gods Are Angry*, which is dull enough to have been subtitled *The Readers Are Angry Too*. Are there well-known mountaineers who have written good fiction? I can think of only one cast-iron candidate – Etienne Bruhl, a G.H.M. member who wrote the wonderful *Accident à la Meije*, a romantic detective novel, and *Variantes*, a collection of superb short stories.[2] Bruhl's characters are well-drawn, we care about their fate, his plots are well-constructed, and mountaineering detail forms an integral part of them. Are there others? Probably not. Perhaps a case can be made for Hamish MacInnes's *Death Reel*, a fast-paced thriller written while the author was recovering from a gangrene infection in 1975. Salkeld and Smith gave it no stars, but it merits one or two. What about *Calculated Risk*? Is it good mountaineering fiction?

In considering the merits of Haston's novel, we have to bear in mind that his death cut it short, leaving only a draft. It has many characters: four climbers, a wise old man, a dozen other briefly-involved men, and six women described rather unkindly by Salkeld and Smith as having 'only one use'. The women and the minor male characters are vague and blurred. John Dunlop, the central character, is Haston himself aged 24 in all but name. Jack McDonald, the second main character, is modelled on John Harlin. The wise old man Charlie Wilson is a close replica of Hamish MacInnes – thus all are borrowed from people well-known to Haston. Despite this, there is a lack of variety: all three share guide-like professional attitudes to climbing, and a somewhat selfish approach to life. It is hard to distinguish Dunlop from McDonald, except that McDonald keeps a dog and tends to call the shots, while Dunlop keeps nothing and plays a rather passive role with McDonald. When together, they are one man, and of one mind – a plot/character error. Dunlop has one surprising un-Haston-like trait bolted on – a taste for classical music. I remember Haston as fond of The Rolling Stones and Bob Dylan, but in Chapter 5 Dunlop is awakened by his girlfriend Judy with coffee and Schumann's *Gesänge der Frühe*, an exquisite piano rarity. Later, he instantly recognizes a Menuhin-Kempff performance of Beethoven's *Kreutzer* Sonata. However, since neither McDonald's dog nor Dunlop's record-player is available at their bivouacs, this small difference of character cannot be effectively exploited.

The plot is simple – a plain narrative of two of Dunlop's climbs and the associated preparations and celebrations. One is in Scotland – a solo ascent of the white wall right of Ossian's Cave in Glencoe – and one on the Jorasses, an ascent in winter of the West Wall of the Walker Spur. This is interrupted by an accident to two 'amateur' climbers, who are bravely rescued by McDonald and Dunlop before they triumphantly complete their ascent. This introduces some uncertainty to the otherwise inevitable progress of the climb, provides an opportunity to demonstrate the technology of Alpine rescue, and serves as a plot device to illuminate the superior competence and judgment of McDonald and Dunlop. Both routes come from Haston's experience: he attempted the white wall with me in 1964, and the route on the Walker with Chris Bonington and Mick Burke.

Despite these weaknesses of character and plot, *Calculated Risk* has two compensating strengths. One is authentic mountaineering detail. Every aspect of both climbs is plausible, the technical methods of the late 60s are painstakingly described and may still provide valuable advice to winter Alpinists. The other is readability. Haston the man did not waste words, and neither did Haston the writer. The pace is relentless. Even a reader whose nose wrinkles at the sketchy characters and thin plot will find it hard to put the book down. So although it falls short of the level set by Bruhl, it was nevertheless a promising effort – page-turners with mountaineering authenticity are rare in mountain fiction. A few more years of exploration with rich and varied characters like Bonington, Scott and Whillans would have provided rocket fuel for any novelist. The avalanche on *La Riondaz* killed a fine mountaineer. But it may well have robbed us of some good mountain fiction too.

1   See their excellent Introduction and Bibliography in *One Step in the Clouds*, Diadem, 1991

2   Thanks to the advocacy of Anne Sauvy, though written long ago, these are both readily available in the Retour à la Montagne collection produced by Editions Hoëbeke.

CHAPTER 1

BREAK-UP

John Dunlop was preoccupied as he negotiated the tricky curves by the side of Loch Lubnaig on the road between Edinburgh and Glencoe. Usually he handled the Honda 750 well, indeed with the same skill and cool which had made him one of Scotland's best mountaineers at the early age of 24, but on this superb September night the machine seemed heavy and difficult to haul round the tight turns. It was his ability for singular concentration that had enabled him to progress along the tricky roads of mountaineering, and slowly the message got to his emotion-filled brain that he should apply the same concentration to handling the bike or he might not see his beloved Glencoe at all. Regaining control over his whirling and violent thoughts he dropped a gear and began to take the corners with his normal skill.

John was angry. Very angry indeed. He had hardly noticed the road between Edinburgh and Stirling because of the dark channels of disillusionment going through his mind.

Earlier that evening he had been sipping a coffee in the University common room, waiting until the rush hour traffic had abated before setting out on the road North, when a tall dark powerfully built figure had sat down rather diffidently across the table.

"Hullo John."

"Well hullo there, George," answered John, slightly surprised at the strange manner. "I thought you'd be home getting your equipment, if you're going to hit the road at the usual time."

George Evans was John's inseparable climbing partner and it was their custom to meet in the pub in Glencoe every Friday night to talk about their weekend's plans. Apart from climbing locally they had also put in four Alpine summer seasons and two winters together, accounting for many of the great Alpine classic climbs and some good first ascents.

"I'm sorry, John, I can't make it this weekend."

Scarcely taking in this unusual statement but with an indefinable feeling that something serious was about to happen, John made a vague attempt at humour to gain time.

"What's up, have you got a new girl friend?"

This was the most bizarre suggestion he could come up with. George had had the same girl friend for seven years. He saw her from time to time, but whenever the question of priorities came up, her or the mountains, it was very evident which side had the upper hand, and to give Jane credit she did not seem to mind. She was proud of George's climbing achievements and was happy enough in his company but at the same time had a string of other boyfriends and Honours English studies to look after.

George did not seem at all amused by this attempt at humour. His heavy body slumped deeper into his chair.

"Jane's in the club, we're going to get married."

John leaned back and looked at his friend in surprise. George's commitment to mountaineering seemed as strong as his own, and when he himself had been in a similar predicament about a year before he and his girlfriend, Pat, had not hesitated to take the necessary action. Assuming the same reaction from George, whom he thought he knew almost as well as himself because of all their common and shared experiences, he shrugged and came back with: "What do you mean, get married? You can get rid of it."

An expression that John had never seen before crept over George's face. There was a touch of dislike, then a kind of sadness, then the familiar stubbornness which he knew only too well, having seen it many times prior to tackling a particularly difficult piece of climbing.

"We don't want to get rid of it. We want to have it," he muttered.

It was John's turn to go through a range of facial emotions: bewilderment at first, then a slightly mocking and knowing smile as he concluded that George was having him on. Often in the past they had confrontations like these, each taking a part that he did not believe in but trying to justify it to the other as if he actually did. Like dialectical fencing matches.

Both found the exercise helpful in developing their reasoning. If you can forcibly defend a position you don't believe in, it makes you much more convincing in the defence of your real beliefs.

Not having taken too much notice of the nuances of mood that had crossed George's face, John came back on a low key to try to baffle him.

"Well, congratulations. I hope the three of you will be happy."

A look of relief came over George's face. "Christ, do you really mean that? I never thought you'd take it so easily. You know it's going to limit my climbing activities. I suddenly realised that I wasn't getting anything from the mountains any more. Since we started five years ago every waking moment and most of my dreams have been taken up by climbing. But I've begun to feel that it's abnormal. Where will I be in another five years—or maybe at the end of next week: a penniless corpse at the foot of a crevasse, remembered only in climbing guide books and pubs where I drank twenty pints and walked out?"

Sitting back, he was about to continue when a small dark-haired girl strolled through the common room and stopped at their table, putting an arm round George.

"Hi Baby. Hi John."

John acknowledged the greeting with a grin and a wave. He was quite impressed by George's outburst: still thinking it was part of the game, he wondered how he could get him to refute it without putting up the expected argument that George, in such good form, would surely demolish. But while he was plotting a more devious attack, Jane forestalled him: "I suppose George's told you the good news about us. I always knew he'd grow out of climbing and settle down. It's about time you and Pat thought of doing the same."

Slowly the realisation dawned on John as the facts forced him to a conclusion that was as welcome as a winter storm on the North Face of the Eiger. These people could be serious. In fact, they were serious. George was getting up, taking his girl's hand and preparing to say something. The self control that had seen John through so many demanding situations broke. He could not think.

"Get stuffed," he ground between his teeth and pushed past the surprised couple.

George held out an arm to try and restrain him, but John was past and gone before he could do anything. His usual calm returned as he turned to the surprised Jane.

"He'll get over it; he's just pissed off that I won't be climbing with him this weekend. We had designs on a new route on Aonach Dubh. Now he'll have to find someone else, but that shouldn't be hard. There are always plenty of good lads hanging around. I'm really looking forward to having a weekend in town for a change. The pubs are open; let's have a pint to start with."

John's Honda was parked in Forest Road which he hit at a run, oblivious of passers-by who turned, surprised, to stare at the rushing figure in leather jacket, jeans and climbing boots clutching a black crash hat.

Angry and confused, he was in the grip of straight reaction. Fortunately he was almost as good a driver as a climber and even in this state he handled the big machine well. But he was fast, way too fast for a city like Edinburgh with its cobbled streets. Catching the lights, in Forest Road he was hitting seventy as he passed the surprised policemen standing at the High Street crossing and had slammed down into second and wound through the tight Bank and Mound corners before they could even think of getting out their notebooks and taking his number.

A faint glimmer of reason started to come through when he started to wind up through the gears down the Mound as he saw the white coated figure standing at the Princes Street intersection. A big white arm was pointed in his direction. He crash-changed down into first, with a howl of protest from the box, and came to a stop before a dour glowering face.

"Where the bluddy hell d'ye think ye'r gaun son?" Then the weather beaten face broke into that rare phenomenon for a police officer—a grin. "Oh, it's you John."

John had passed him every Friday night on and off for the last two years and they had established a kind of rapport. John's cheery chat helped take his mind off the honking congestion, and the hordes of office faces hurrying home on a Friday night.

"Ye'd better slow doon. At that rate ye'll never get tae the West End, far less Glencoe and if the Inspector sees ye, ye'll be spending the weekend in the High Street instead of wandering around these bluddy hills. Although it might be a good thing for ye, keep ye safe!"

Despite his anger, some of John's natural good humour forced itself to the fore as the dead-pan policeman waved him on with a "Away ye go and look after yeself."

"I'll try hard, Wullie," he grinned, kicking into gear, and gunned off.

This brief interlude kept him at a reasonable speed through the city till he reached the quietness of the Stirling road, where the images of his closest friend and their conversation began to crowd in. The speedometer needle crept up as the bike seemed to drive itself.

By the time he had passed the twisting side of Loch Lubnaig, the anger had gone and only a resentful perplexity remained, for with his characteristic logical clarity he had decided that it was much better to concentrate on driving as he would have all weekend to think about the problem. He just could not believe that five years of sharing the complex intensity of every conceivable type of mountaineering experience had come to an end just because of a girl and what could only have been a drunken slip on George's behalf. But already, almost subconsciously, he had begun to adjust to the fact that George was going out of his life, for he always looked ahead. There would be much analysis, self-searching and motive-seeking but basically the hard conclusion was emerging: that once anyone showed any slip in his dedication he could only fall by the wayside. John enjoyed many pleasures in life but climbing was the only thing that gave him more than momentary satisfaction. Any partner had to share this outlook or ascents could be put in jeopardy. Second only to the frightened person on a mountain is the person who is wondering why he is there. Both are potentially lethal companions. The climbs that John was doing demanded nearly everything from himself and his partner. There was just not enough left for continually watching over someone else.

With these thoughts tumbling around in the small part of his mind that was not occupied by driving, he was going fast and well now: Tyndrum floated past and he dropped a gear below the cross roads for the long steady climb up to the flat out straights of Rannoch Moor.

As he glanced up to make sure no errant brewery lorry was coming non-stop out of the Oban road—he had almost been caught out before by one whose driver had obviously spent all day drinking as well as delivering and was rushing home for Friday night—he caught sight of a red rucsac and a slim blond figure in well fitting Levis and blue parka standing with a thumb out. A flash of recognition cleared his thoughts as he scrutinised the hitchhiker.

"It's Judy Scott. I'll give her a lift across the moor." Once again the much tried gearbox whined and protested as he whipped down into first and drew up, wheels locked, beside her...

A pair of cool blue eyes smiled a greeting from under the blond fringe. "What are you in such a rush for? The pub'll still be open and Aonach Dubh hasn't fallen down."

Laughing a welcome despite his troubled state, John gestured to the pillion seat. "Get on, if you dare and I'll tell you about it over a pint when we get there."

Hopping on lithely Judy tossed him a grin as she adjusted her rucsac to rest on top of John's, strapped on the pannier.

"O.K. Let's go, ace."

Resting her hands lightly on the back pannier she relaxed back as John took off up the hill.

Braking heavily he took the left hander at the top fast, impressed by the way his passenger leaned with the bike and did not clutch at his waist with both arms, as most women passengers did. With the beautiful straights of Rannoch Moor ahead, John wound into top, set the Honda on course at around 95-100, sat back and began to think about his passenger.

The quarrel with George dimmed fast, for Judy was that unusual combination: a good-looking woman and a climber. Not only was she good-looking, she could easily have been called extremely attractive. Blond hair cut very short, fine features, smallish breasts, lean hips and long legs which had propelled her up some of the most difficult climbs in Scotland. She was a year younger than John and had been around the Scottish climbing scene as long as John could remember. They were casual good friends and had argued many a beer away over the respective merits of different philosophical systems, both being students of that very discussable subject but at different Universities, John at Edinburgh, Judy at Glasgow. There had never been anything more in their relationship, mainly because Judy had been living for the last three years with Don McPhee, who was considerably older than she, also a very good climber but one who because of his application to his work had never climbed much outside Scotland. John respected his abilities but they were not close friends.

Slightly puzzled as to why Judy was alone and hitchhiking, as she usually travelled up with Don in his car, he throttled back till they were cruising at a leisurely sixty and flung the question back over his shoulder.

"Where's Don?"

Coming up from her huddle behind his back Judy cupped a hand to his ear. "He had to go to London for a conference and Glasgow felt dreary and dull so I decided to wander up the Glen to do a little climbing."

John nodded, momentarily swerved to avoid a sheep lying on the road and wound back the throttle again. They could talk at leisure quite soon. A few thoughts that the absent Don might not have approved crept into his mind. He did not know if he would try to do anything about it. He did not know if Judy would feel that way anyway. But where good-looking girls are concerned, speculation is inevitable.

As he rounded the corner at the top of Black Mount, a view appeared that routed all other thoughts. He had seen it many times before, in many types of conditions, but it never failed to give a tug to the part of his mind that dealt with aesthetic appreciation. Before them, the entrance to Glencoe lay in blue-black shadow in the retreating daylight with the bulk of Buachaille Etive Mor, The Great Shepherd, looming up on the left, hiding in its darkening rocks relics of experiences of generations of climbers.

Quickly it was no more as John filed the vision, turned on his lights and geared down fast for the entrance to the road leading to Kingshouse Hotel. Down the narrow road, watch-

ing for the gleaming eyes of sleeping sheep; bouncing over the
bridge; sudden silence as he cut the motor before the welcoming hotel.

Judy clambered off, wiping wind-driven tears from her high
cheek bones. Pulling off his crash hat and goggles, and wiping
dirt from his mouth, John gave her an appreciative glance as
she stood shaking out her ruffled hair. He was about to say
something light-hearted in the usual bantering tone they used
towards each other, when the black remembrance of his parting with George rushed in like a winter storm on Mont Blanc.
He turned to go into the bar: "Let's go, I need that pint."

With quick feminine sensitivity Judy caught the brief flash
and change of mood but decided to say nothing. Thoughtfully she followed him. From the gentle silence of the highland
night, stepping through the door into the crowded bar was
like coming on to a Fellini film set. A newly-fed fire was
flickering into flame, showering sparks up an open fireplace.
There was a smell of much used human bodies. Most of the
groups were standing around muttering intently, clutching
large pint mugs of beer, but in one of the corners a highly
competitive darts game was in action.

John elbowed his way through the door, nodding and passing a few words with most people as he did so. In this tightly
knit climbing community everyone knew everything about
everyone else. But the fierce rivalries of climbing were always
to the fore, and groups constantly formed, dissolved and
reformed according to climbing attitudes. There was also the
traditional rivalry between East and West, which sometimes
even exploded into violence in the volatile atmosphere of the
bar.

Returning with a couple of lagers, John found himself
shouting above the noise. But he was in no mood for an
extended conversation about weather conditions and what to
climb, as would surely develop if they stayed by the bar.

"Let's go through to the lounge where we can at least hear
what we're saying," he said, his mouth close to Judy's ear.
She nodded and they slipped through into the hotel lounge
bar, the exact antithesis of the climbers' bar: deep armchairs,
hushed, with only a few tweed-clad shepherds drinking from
large amber coloured glasses at the bar.

They sat down in one of the far corners. Judy, sipping her drink, addressed John in a teasing manner: "Well, well, what's wrong with you, quitting the bar? You usually can't wait to hear the current gossip and to find out the bad reports people have been giving about second ascents of some of your new routes. Where's Georgie Boy? He usually manages to beat you here by a few minutes. You think he's driven that beast of a machine into the loch?"

George owned a 1000 cc Vincent Black Shadow. A connoisseur's motor bike, long out of production but having the status of something like a pre-war Bugatti, it was one of the most powerful things man had ever put on two wheels.

Noticing the shadow that came over John's face, she dropped the bantering tone and addressed him sharply: "What the hell's wrong with you anyway? You're as uptight as I've ever seen you. Has someone pinched your little lady?" Then she reverted to her natural good humour. "Might not be a bad idea. Could give someone else a chance!"

Giving her a sharply speculative look and storing this remark for future consideration, John contemplated the pro's and con's of telling Judy about the quarrel. He usually kept his problems very closely to himself but he knew the word would soon be abroad. George was also a friend of Judy's. Leaning forward and looking straight at her, he said: "George has quit."

A startled look shot through her eyes, but this was the only indication she gave of having heard. Being an intelligent listener, she knew there was more to come, that John would tell her as much as he wanted to, and that questions from her would not elicit any more information.

Briefly, in a low savage monotone, John told the story of the afternoon's meeting. Judy listened silently with an air of abstraction. She knew this had to come out, but at the same time her quick mind was sorting and evaluating. With her philosophical training, she had acquired a characteristic not found in many feminine minds—the ability to conduct logical thought processes. Coming to an end of the bare and, to him, bad facts of the matter, John continued straight into a highly critical analysis of George's behaviour.

"Where could he suddenly have gone wrong? Surely a person like him couldn't change his life-style in the space of a week?" These were rhetorical questions. Judy stayed silent. John continued: "And you know we've just had one hell of an Alpine season: did the Eiger Norwand and the North Face Direct of the Droites. And more. George was going really well. We shared everything. Lots of hard moments, but he never never lost his cool. Often it was his needling that got me going in the morning: I hate early starts, but George was always wide awake and thrusting away, knowing that I'd get into shape when the sun rose. There was no indication that he was tiring of climbing, even one little bit, far less considering quitting!" He took a long pull at his glass: "If he'd said he was getting tired of pushing at that level I could have understood. Christ, you've really got to be into climbing to continue pushing and pushing. But to say he wants to quit for such trivial reasons . . ." Grimacing, John made a gesture of disgust and was about to continue his diatribe when Judy cut in quietly:

"And what's so wrong about wanting to get married, with a child on the way? Have you thought of Jane and how she feels? Do you really know what it is for a girl to have an abortion? Sure, you forced Pat to have one, but did you really care about her feelings? No. All you could see was something that might interfere with your climbing. You're a fanatic, John; you can't see outside the range of your own single field."

Giving her a hard glance, John prepared to cut in but Judy raised her hand in a "let me continue" gesture and carried on.

"No, don't get angry. You're angry enough with George but maybe it should be the other way round. Just let me say what has been obvious for the last year—not only to me but to other people as well. You've been so locked into your climbing that you've failed to see how much you use people. There's only one really important thing in your mind and that's to be a world-class climber. In fact you're almost there already. Personally, I like and admire what you've done, but what I don't like is this lack of feeling for others. You'd tread on anything or anyone to get what you want."

John sat alert and listening. In his many previous discussions with Judy they had never got down to this basic personal level but he knew her well enough to know that her opinions would be lucid, sincere and deeply felt, worthy of his respect even though he might dislike and disagree with them. John did not mind being attacked verbally. To have to defend himself in this fashion kept him sharp witted and there was no doubt that he would have to defend strongly by the time Judy was finished, as she showed no sign of slowing down.

Her emotion showing only in the slight narrowing of her blue eyes as she concentrated on John, she carried on calmly: "Take George, for example: everyone but you has been aware that you're the driving force in the partnership. He's a brilliant climber, sure, but if it hadn't been for you, I'm sure he would never have reached the standard he has. The force of your personality and his friendship for you has kept him going this long but did you take a long look at him when you came back from the Alps? Obviously not. He was tense, withdrawn, not the old relaxed George. You got the feeling that he had been forcing himself along and that he was on the brink of nervous exhaustion. This incident with Jane probably came as a welcome relief, a way out. Knowing George, he'll probably make a go of it. But can't you see it was the only way to tell you he wanted out? It had to be something drastic like that: you'd never have believed him if he'd just come up and said he wanted out. He was smart enough and humble enough to make a direct break. You should at least respect him for that. There's no reason why you should not be friends even though he is no longer your climbing partner. For the sake of all you've experienced together, you owe him that. He's quit. There's no way you're going to change that. Even if you do try and persuade him, a reluctant partner's no use: I've climbed enough to know that. Treat him as a friend. If you don't, he's going to be unhappy for a long time because he thinks so much of you. You know that."

Sitting back, she relaxed a little and a brief smile crossed her face. "Don't take me for an interfering bitch. I've been aware of this for some time but I'd never have dared say anything unless what I'd suspected could happen hadn't turned into actual fact."

Giving her a long steady look, John sifted methodically through the points that Judy had made.

"You've made a lot of good points but what you have said sums up two points of view: the woman's and the casual climber's." Judy flashed him a sharp glance. "Now don't you get annoyed! You're certainly a woman and you're a good climber too. But climbing's just a passing phase with you. You love coming away at weekends, you like the mountains, you like the climbing company: but you could give it up without too many regrets. When you go to Europe in summer you spend as much time in Florence as you do in Chamonix. For you it's one of the dozens of beautiful facets of life that are there to be enjoyed: it doesn't rule your life as it does mine. I'd love to go to Florence and Sienna but every moment the sun shone I wouldn't be able to enjoy the paintings and architecture for fear the sky was blue over Mont Blanc and I was missing the chance to do one of the great climbs. Maybe you're right, maybe I'm obsessive. But Jackie Stewart didn't become world champion just by pottering around vaguely in cars. He had one singular urge and that was to be the best Formula 1 driver in the world. Racing was his life, just as climbing is my life. Of course, in climbing there's no such thing as the number one climber. There are so many different facets of the sport that there's no single person who's the best in all of them. But there is a group that's recognised as the world's best and that's where I want to be. God knows I'm far enough away from it now, but I'd never have the remotest chance of reaching it with your attitude. It's difficult for most people to understand a singular strong urge to do something well. You only really take out of something the amount you put in; you get small amounts of pleasure out of many things, whereas I get a huge amount of pleasure out of one.

I think my way is the best for me at heart. You think your way is best, but not only for you! In the last few minutes you were trying to convert me. Why? I can understand your way of thinking because I've passed through that stage, but you'll never really be able to understand mine. Yet you presume to judge it merely from the effects it has on other people, which, because they're of your frame of mind, can sometimes be unpleasant."

John paused to take a sip of his forgotten lager while Judy

fumed with rage. She could never agree with him. What he was saying subtly was that she should not talk about things she did not really know about. She found his arrogance maddening. He seemed to be putting himself on a higher pedestal, but the revelations about his reasons for climbing were intriguing.

He continued: "Take George for example. One of my principal emotions is disappointment in him. I don't like to see a strong person becoming weak. I'll just qualify this before you explode. Doing normal things like getting married and having children isn't weakness for the normal person, but it is for George. Despite all you say about his being unhappy. It was surface observation. He was good and I know he was experiencing the great happiness that comes from doing one thing really well. There's no lying in extreme climbing, either to yourself or to your partner. He had to be happy and wanting to do the things we were doing only a month ago, or he couldn't have done them. He was every bit as good as I was and the reason why I'm disappointed and puzzled—'cause that's what I am more than anything else now—is that I can't see why someone should give up so much for so little. The so little he could have had any time. The so much took a lot of striving to get and now he's thrown it away."

This unusual outburst was having its effect slowly, and he was winding down.

"I'll always be friendly with George but something's gone for ever. Maybe he's happy, but I'll never be able to see why." His normal coolness returned. "Thank you for provoking me, Judy. I've thrown out a few things that I haven't often put into words. Maybe you should go and talk to some of the others now: think about tomorrow, and what to climb. 'Begone dull care', eh?"

Her good humour returned and, feeling almost privileged to have heard a brief glimpse of John's philosophy, she decided the subject was closed. He had been accurate in what he said and in his description of her behaviour, but had been wrong on one count. She had wanted to be amongst the world's best woman climbers. She was good, but in her self-critical way she had realised that she was not good enough. Slowly she had turned away until, although it was something she really enjoyed, it was only one of her many interests.

As well as being a good philosopher, she was a good psychologist and recognised that John, in his present mood, was not going to be interested in any of her old problems. She switched tracks.

"Where are you staying tonight?"

John was still slightly abstracted. "I was going to go to the club cottage at Lagangarbh but I don't really feel like talking to groups. I've got my tent with me: I think I'll go and camp beneath the Buachaille on Gunpowder Green." He added mischievously: "I hear you're a good cook. Do you want to — er — chat a little more?"

This was by no means the proposition it sounded, tent sharing between male and female climbers without any sexual connotations being common. However, in this case anything was possible: from the laughing looks they exchanged and their previous conversations they were both aware of the beginnings of something more than their previous casual friendship.

"Let's go then," Judy replied. "I don't know about the cooking but I think I'd prefer canvas to a crowded hut too."

Quietly they slipped out of the bar, leaving the scene, changed only in time with the tweed-suited figures still muttering, the amber-coloured glasses full again, the fire still flickering.

The clear cool autumn night was dark and moonless. Only the bulk of the Buachaille blotted out the stars as they drew up in the layby where the path to the proposed campsite began. Grabbing packs, they stumbled torchless along the vague track amongst the heather till they came to the river.

John broke the silence: "It can't have rained much this week, the river's pretty low." He set off jumping the stepping stones followed by the nimble Judy.

That particular night they were lucky, for after a day of rain the river Etive, fed by most of the mountain streams in the glen, can become a fast flowing monster, making the crossing a real and sometimes impossible problem.

The small patch of flat grass on the other side was deserted. Hastily pitching the tent they felt like the only people in a tiny universe bordered by the gently-flowing river and the gently watching Buachaille. Somehow as they sat under canvas their thoughts turned to a subject more pleasurable than cooking, and soon their worlds and thoughts were joined in a fusion so complete that even the insistent murmur of the river by their ears went unnoticed.

CHAPTER 2

GLENCOE

The cry of a peewit brought the purple dawn through the tent flap. Soft clear mornings in Glencoe are as rare as genuine Ming vases, fine mist, horizontal rain, clinging sleet or fast moving snow being more usual. The area is so close to the west coast of Scotland that bad weather is the norm, and thereby hangs the sombre beauty that many know and love. But with the sun comes renaissance, the blacks and greys appearing as purples and subtle velvety greens, and the rivers running clear and gentle, looking as if they could never rush, dark brown and full of menace through the Glen.

It was such a morning as John blinked into freshness. A day for climbing. As really fine days are so rare it is usually only the aficionados who profit by them. Patiently coming freetime upon freetime their commitment is finally blessed by inheritance. It is on these rare good days or even rarer good spells that the new and difficult climbing is done. Sometimes a non-regular is lucky, but rarely. John, who had been on hand for most of the good periods in the previous three years, had left his unmistakeable mark on the cliffs of the Glen.

Climbing rocks seems a futile pastime to many. But is it so futile in a century during which the different human races have spent the best part of their time trying mutually to annihilate each other?

Lying quietly with his head out of the tent door John thought of his American friends who he occasionally climbed with in the Alps. Passionate believers in peace, many had fled their native country and were now cut off from friends, relatives, wives and families because they did not believe in dying in Vietnamese paddyfields to gratify the ambitions of corrupt politicians. There was no questioning their courage. It had been proved time and time again in their chosen form of conflict, the perennial one between man and nature. Climbing is not a war between man and mountain. You try to live in harmony with the natural environment. But when the environment is alien, often hostile and seldom friendly you must be prepared to fight to find your way. In this type of fight you do not destroy. It is not a negative thing. You gain respect for the awesome power of natural forces and you also have time to take a long look at yourself. Nature seems to have a mind; if you don't match up you are quickly rejected. But if you attack with respect and caution it is usually possible to come through the worst that natural forces can throw at you, though often only just, for their defences are exceedingly powerful.

A movement beside him chased away these reflections and a tousled blond head appeared in the opening. Neither alluded to what had passed the night before. Deep discussion and lovemaking were normal events in their lives.

"I don't need to tell you what a great morning it is," she said. "I didn't tell you last night but I've made an arrangement with Cathy Gates to go and try one of the hard ones— the East buttress of Aonach Dubh." She smiled, "Chauvinistic women, you know, both of us have done harder things in male company, but this time we want to try it on our own. It'd be the first time a serious Scottish climb had been done by all female rope. What are you going to do Johnny boy?" Mischievously she teased: "You can join us if you want but you wouldn't be allowed to lead."

John burst out laughing. "And you accuse me of being ambitious. Thanks for the kind offer but I don't want to get half way up a climb with two twittering women's libbers who come to pieces and then want me to drag them up. Seriously though, the best of luck—I've done all the climbs there a couple of times; they're hard. You're both good, but remember a lot of your difficult climbs have been done as seconds. It gets lonely out in front sometimes. I'm going to have a look at the wall to the right of Ossian's Cave. George and I had a couple of goes at it but been driven off by rain once and darkness the next. I think I'll sniff around on my own."

A worried shadow crossed Judy's face, but she kept her thoughts to herself, saying: "Have fun, but if you're going there you can give me a ride: I said I'd meet Cathy about eight. She's staying at Charlie Wilson's."

As she started to brew the morning tea, she mulled over what John had said. The cliff to the right of Ossian's Cave was one of the hardest pieces of unclimbed rock left in the Glen. Good climbers had been getting rebuffed constantly in the last few years. To attack it alone was very bold indeed. True, he had said that he was only going to look at it but she knew what that meant.

Soloing is the most dangerous and committing type of climbing. Although there are methods of protection using back ropes and mechanical clamps instead of partners, they are vastly inferior to the solidity of another body. Psychologically it is also wearing. There is no-one to talk to on the stance or to hold you if you fall. Self-control has to be very strong to halt the many fears which come floating into mind. You need to be very calm to contemplate a solo climb, and Judy was worried that he was being driven to it by his quarrel with George, as a kind of angry gesture. Judging by his previous night's conversation he did not seem like that, but any vestige of emotional thinking could be detrimental to the frame of mind needed to complete difficult solo ascents.

John seemed to read her mind as he munched a huge bacon-stuffed roll. "I know what you're thinking, but don't. I've thought about a major solo climb for a long time. If George had been here I'd have been morally committed to try the climb with him, but now it seems as if the time and occasion have been given to me." He finished his tea. "That was a good breakfast. Are you ready? My gear's still on the bike; we can sort it out down at Charlie's."

Charlie was a writer and mountain photographer who had bought a cottage in Glencoe, on one of the rare available pieces of land. A fine climber, he had wandered through most of the major mountain ranges in the world at one time or another, taking beautiful black and white pictures and writing humorously about different cultures. At fifty he had settled into Glencoe, living fairly comfortably on the proceeds of his books and attempting to do that thing that most writers of fact want to try at least once—write a novel. He had a great rapport with younger climbers. On the few occasions they managed to persuade him to go out, flashes of his old ability enabled him to play such games as arriving at the top of a difficult pitch with a few coils of rope in his hand, muttering about the possibilities of climbing the moves in nailed boots.

At present the hordes of younger climbers, skipping up difficult rock in their specially-made light rubber soled boots, tended to forget the difficult things that had been done by their elders in clumsy tricouni nailed boots. Charlie took every opportunity he could to remind them of the fact. Basically loving younger company he had installed four bunks and cooking facilities in a small barn behind his cottage. A favoured few friends gathered here most weekends and it was here that Judy was to meet her climbing partner Cathy Gates.

Cathy was a few years older than Judy, and was a tough independent woman. After graduating in English at Edinburgh, she had taken off for the States and Canada to do as much climbing and skiing as possible. Not really beautiful but attractive to men she had done the full circuit from living under polythene in Yosemite Valley to sharing a film star's ski lodge in Aspen, Colorado. But she never got deeply involved, and developed her climbing skills to the extent that even in the rat-race of climbing competition in the Western States, good climbers had taken to asking her to go and climb instead of going to bed. Now she was back in Britain hoping to start work on a Ph.D.

Charlie's cottage was about ten miles down the Glen and as they strolled across to where the Honda was parked, they could see signs of life appearing on the road. Vehicles of all types, mostly beaten up old vans and motor bikes of various sizes and shapes began to cruise down the road, which was filling with people, ropes and rucsacs. The transient climbing population was emerging from its multiplicity of holes, like marmots at the first sign of spring. Whistling and noisy, the crowd passed by, occasionally waving, grateful for the fact that Glencoe had granted them a fine day.

"Christ," said John "the classics are going to be crowded today. It's a good job we're going to secluded places. Oh-oh, here comes trouble!"

A red mini-Cooper S four-wheel drifted round the corner

before their parking place, and was about to scream off up the straight when its driver caught sight of them, trod on the brakes, and came to a rubber-annihilating stop beside them. The passenger window rattled down and a thick Mancunian accent floundered out into the foreign air.

"Well now, John Dunlop and Judy Scott, what have you two been up to?"

"And what's worse, where are you heading?" The second voice came from the long, lean bespectacled driver who unwound himself from the cramped seat of the little car and, stretching, continued in a drawling English public school accent: "It looks as if they should be selling tickets to get on to the climbs."

Nodding a greeting, John parried in that tone of voice that can only be used with old friends: "There's going to be enough pollution in our air with the North Sea Oil without having foreigners climbing in Glencoe. What's wrong, can't you get anything hard enough to satisfy you in Wales?"

The driver answered easily: "We thought we'd take some time off from the competition down there and come to a more relaxed atmosphere and some easier climbing. A few days off, you might say."

The two Englishmen, Mark Jones the driver and Tom Widnes were in the top rank of British climbers. During the summer they had teamed up to make a foursome with John and George on the North Face of the Droites, in Chamonix. John knew that they were not here to look at the scenery and easier climbs, but he also knew that no amount of questioning would bring out their objective unless they wanted to tell him. For a moment he suspected that they might be going for the same objective as himself but his fears were chased away as Widnes took up the conversation.

"We've been looking for you. We want to try the second ascent of that route you did on Gearr Aonach with George. You seem to think it was quite hard, didn't you?"

John nodded but didn't speak, as Mark cut in: "Can you tell us where it goes and we'll be off? Can't waste a good day in Scotland."

John gave them a description but, when asked where he was going, named a classic and said he was going to do it with

Judy. They looked slightly surprised but nodded as they climbed back into the car.

"Thanks, we'll see you in the pub tonight," they chorused and took off rapidly down the Glen.

Turning to Judy, John said: "Hope you didn't mind the lie but I didn't want that pair to be aware of Ossian's Cave. If I fail today they'd be up there in a flash tomorrow."

Judy grinned. "All right by me, lad. I don't want the Sassenachs grabbing our routes either. Shall we get moving?"

Jumping on the bike, they drove at a leisurely pace through the Glen, past the Three Sisters of Glencoe, Beinn Fhada, Gearr Aonach and Aonach Dubh, turning off left beneath the latter and taking the rough track for half a mile to where Charlie's cottage, white against the heather and cliffs, was reflected in the shallows of Loch Achtriochton. Charlie's tall figure was standing at the gate.

"Well, surprise surprise. Didn't expect to see you, John. Hello Judy. How are you both?"

"Good form, Charlie," answered John, shaking hands while Judy gave him a hug.

"Cathy's just making some tea; will you have a cup before you rush off? I hear there's ambitious projects in the air, for the ladies at least. And where are you heading today?"

Knowing that anything he said would be safe with Charlie, John told him briefly what had happened and where he was going.

Charlie nodded straight faced. "Aye, well, take care. You'll never be able to live it down if I have to come up and rescue you. You could never afford enough whisky for the rescue fees." Then, more sombrely: "It's a pity about George."

He fell silent, knowing better than to pursue what could only be a difficult subject for John who in turn did not elaborate but said laughingly: "Just for that reason, Charlie, I'll be super careful. Anyway it's time I was going if I'm going to get anywhere today. I'll just say hello to Cathy then get moving."

At that moment Cathy came running out of the cottage and gave him a crushing hug.

"Hi, Johnny boy."

"Hello Cathy, you'd better save your strength for your

climb today." Turning quickly and jumping on the bike he gunned off, shouting a quick goodbye.

Charlie and the two girls looked pensively at the retreating figure then at each other, until Charlie broke the silence: "If anyone can do it he can, but I think I'll go down beneath Aonach Dubh with a book and some cold beer and my binoculars. I may as well take advantage of the sunshine in my own peculiar way."

Judy looked gratefully at him. "Thanks Charlie. There's no reason why we should worry about him. As you say, if anyone can solo that wall it's him, but the fact that you're keeping a sly old eye on him makes me feel a lot more relaxed. Means I should be able to perform better on our little project. Eh Cathy?"

Nodding agreement Cathy looked contemplatively into the distance.

"Yeah. He's good and in a different class from us but it makes you wonder if anyone can be strong enough to push through the ideas he has. He's one of my favourite people, Johnny, but sometimes I wonder if he doesn't ask too much of himself and the people around him." She turned to Judy. "I've been around the best in the States and know that nothing gets between them and their mountains. Girlfriends included. Don't get too involved, Judy. I know you can look after yourself but that 'adoring' tender look you gave him spells ill."

Judy merely laughed. "Don't get philosophical on me: I only listened to his problems. Even the most self-contained person has to talk about them sometimes. I think we're going to have enough trouble with our own particular problem to-day. Shall we get going?"

Cathy laughed. "Sorry, guess I've been around Americans too long. Always wanting to solve other people's problems or seeing problems where none exist. Let's have a cup of tea and get off up the hill."

Charlie, noticing this little female altercation, shrewdly kept silent, put an arm round each of their shoulders and ushered them into the cool of the stone kitchen. It was still only 8 a.m. but already a hazy heat was beginning to rise from the heather.

CHAPTER 3

A SOLO CLIMB

John slid the bike gently to a halt beneath the squat mass of Aonach Dubh. Ossian's Cave was very obvious, a dark slit stuck in the middle of a cliff where a fugitive highlander was once supposed to have hidden from pursuing Englishmen. Having been in the cave, he personally doubted this tale: the floor was a very steep shelf with not too many ledges and the approach involved two hundred feet of moderate climbing up vertical grass, heather and rock. But his thoughts were not on the cave itself but on the wall to its right, which gleamed white against the black of the cave, standing out amongst the darkness of the surrounding rock.

Many eyes had seen this glistening piece of whiteness, an unusual colour among Glencoe's predominantly sombre shades of rock, but it was a long time before anyone got round to trying to set foot on it. There had been one attempt in the fifties by Bryce and Hesketh, two excellent climbers of the time; they hardly touched the wall. Struggling all day, they managed a bare hundred feet and retreated, pronouncing it nearly unclimbable. This had sufficiently deterred people until recently when it had been the scene of a few determined but unsuccessful attempts, John and George having made the best. Each time they made a considerable advance, and each time the Glencoe rainstorms had come howling in to force them into bedraggled retreats from small stances. There were no ledges to speak of on the five hundred foot cliff. At the end of each rope length there was usually nothing but a tiny placement for the front part of their feet.

The pitches they had already done were very hard but John felt in such good shape that he reckoned he could free solo them—climbing without any rope protection whatsoever. The last two hundred feet leaned back into some roofs, which looked like he would have to make use of self protection methods.

With thoughts and turmoils of the previous evening behind him, John was thinking ahead, not back, sifting through the problems to come as he methodically packed his rucsac. It was going to be heavy because he was carrying what would normally be taken by two people. Two 50 metre 9 mm perlon ropes, P.A.s, the special light rock shoes, karabiners and pitons.

He set off across level heather at first. It led to the steep narrow track to the cave. As he moved up the rest of the Glen slowly fell away behind him until all that was left in front was the shadowy slit of Ossian's Cave, the white wall and the long section of dark difficult rock stretching further rightwards out of sight. He felt fit, relaxed and, as a good indication of his calm state of mind, was thinking about the unclimbed part and how he would tackle it rather than what would happen if he fell off. The moment a solo climber begins to think about the consequence of a fall it's time for him to turn back and go home. He decided that, assuming he could climb the first three rope lengths, he would tackle the unknown part using a safety rope.

In solo climbing, this means a lot of hard work. You tie yourself on to one end of the rope as usual but in place of the second man the other end goes to a bunch of pitons. You then set off placing pitons normally but using jumar clamps to shorten the fall distance. Once you have reached the top of the pitch, you have to abseil back down taking out the pitons, jumar up the rope again to the upper stance, and pull the ropes up to make a new start.

As he approached the cave and moved from sunlight into shadow, John could not help but think of the rest of the climbers in the Glen. Everywhere there would be happy shouting as people tackled the well known problems. The usual competitions, the rivalries, the girls lying in the grass lazily watching. John could not understand the climbers who could only perform to an audience and in the small world of Glencoe rock climbing. There were so many who did just play at it, climbing well but at a low level, satisfied with the applause of the waiting ladies, the admiring looks in the bar, and the easily shared sleeping bag after. Climbers like this were aplenty but ephemeral. Here today, gone tomorrow to another interest—like George, he thought in a sudden flash. He knew that in making this analogy he was wrong but the puzzlement continued, for it seemed that from different beginnings George had reached a similar end.

Realising he was losing his concentration John shut off the subject as he looked at the white wall only a few feet from his nose.

There they were, the old familiar features. A line of shadowy grooves leading up to beneath the roofs, each holding a part of his life where he had had to struggle and search into his capabilities to the exclusion of exterior factors. But each time the exterior factors had come sweeping in, dismissing with a casual impersonal stroke his superb inward control and sending him fleeing downwards in torrents of rain and sleet.

The whiteness of the rock was illusory. Face to face, it was a light grey, covered in many places by the whitish dead-looking lichen which spreads like dandruff over the places climbers rarely go. Dry, it is harmless and only gets in your eyes. Wet, it is a serious rival, sending the rubbered feet of the climber skidding and sliding and tempting him away from his avowed intent of staying on the rock.

John remembered his previous encounters and automatically gave a glance to the sky. No problems there. The sky was holding deep blue against the greens and browns of Aonach Eagach and distant Ben Nevis. Changing into his rock shoes, he made his last mental check. Temptations crept in. He could easily turn back. No one would blame him. He could say it looked too dangerous for solo climbing. The trusted few who knew where he was would believe him. No one could ever say he had made a cowardly decision: what he had already accomplished was proof of his ability. If they knew of this attempt many might think he had lost the sense of perspective and judgement that had made him into the climber he was at present. Here he might be encroaching on the suicidal, the infamous 'death wish' so loosely thrown about by non-climbers in conversations about climbers.

An analysis of his subconscious motives was creeping through, but John had no wish to indulge in one of his Zen type habits of lying around letting thoughts evolve and evaluating them. He knew what he wanted to do. A great experience lay in front of him amongst the intricate cracks of the grey rock. His mind was open and waiting, his body relaxed and ready.

Leaving his sac tucked under a rock, he tied into the two ropes, slung the hardware around him, took a calculating look at the first moves, rubbed his P.A.s against the rock to take off any vestiges of mud, and started to climb.

Watching a good climber at work is a very special thing. There was no audience watching John, but had he been performing for television, the layman would probably have lost interest quickly. Hard rock calls for positive, calculated movements, often slow. There is no flashing upwards with gay abandon, with the abyss ever deepening below. Some climbers size up the situations quickly then move. Others go up and down exploring all possibilities before involving themselves in any degree of commitment. John could not afford any mistakes: there was no one holding his rope, no piton to clip into.

About twenty feet up he came to the first difficulties. He was straddling a groove which suddenly reared into a crack with a horizontal overhanging start. Relaxing as much as was possible on his small holds, he recalled his previous ascents of these pieces of rock. It was a committing move, called an undercut layback, where you stick your hands behind an up-cutting but level crack, bring your feet up parallel to them until you are hanging out by opposing pressure systems, then proceed along the crack in this extremely tiring fashion until the outer edge is reached. Then one hand must be brought out of the undercling and, with the other holding all the body weight, must jam in the vertical crack sufficiently well for you to transfer all the weight temporarily into that crack. Even then it was not finished. Less exhausting perhaps than the undercut laybacking, there was fifteen feet of very strenuous jamming with arms and legs before a ledge could be reached. There was no resting on the undercut part. You either climbed it or fell off.

Emptying his mind of all other things John faced the overhang. There were similar difficulties above but the first one is always the worst. The strain on the body is obvious, and the mind must be wound up to a sufficient extent to sustain a lot of punishment. Being alone, John was calm. He thought of nothing else. Staring hard at the crack line, he refreshed his memory with a searching glance and moved smoothly into action. Within a minute it was all over. On the ledge he let out his breath with a great sigh. He had wound himself in and out of the danger zone so quickly that it scarcely seemed to have happened, but already he was planning ahead. A touch of loneliness came and went. Usually after such a passage, you relax and relieve the tension by shouting to your partner or singing. For John there was only the unattached rope trailing behind, the rock rearing up ahead and the quietness of the Glen.

As far as involvement with the rock is concerned, he was totally alone, but if telepathic moral support is capable of being given, it was beaming in slowly from a sheltered rocky inlet beside the river. Charlie had followed at leisure down the Glen and was now ensconced in one of his favourite spots, a small incut balcony above the river just before it went careening violently towards the gorge and the meeting of the Three Waters. There was room for two people to stretch out, and it was completely hidden from the road, but above all it gave an uninterrupted view of Aonach Dubh and especially the white wall to the right of Ossian's Cave. Charlie had brought a book along but it lay untouched beside him. A pair of powerful binoculars resting on a small tripod brought John up as close as on a television screen. Charlie knew the wall's reputation, having listened to John and George discussing their previous attempts. Despite the calm face that studied the wall methodically, he was worried. His mountaineering experience was wide and varied, but had never been totally dominated by the singular urge to climb more and more difficult things. His fierce love for mountaineering was many-faceted: as well as hard climbs, he enjoyed taking pictures, wandering alone over easy peaks, going for long ski tours and, when all was done, sitting down and writing about mountains. He knew there were a lot of people passionately interested in mountains who for various reasons would never have the chance to sample them. Having been lucky enough to have wandered through most of the world's great ranges, he got great pleasure from being able to pass on some of his enjoyment through photography and writing.

Studying John as he rested on the first stance, having completed the first pitch, Charlie wondered about the boy's make-up. Was such a talent and such an urge something that John had developed completely independently or were there other factors at work? What drove a healthy, intelligent and apparently normal 24-year-old to walk with death in such a way? Because this was what John was doing. You can only gloss over the facts so much, and in reality any false move on his behalf incurred a high probability of death or serious injury. Sadly Charlie thought of his friends who had been killed while climbing. There had been one or two as talented as John but their burning drive had led them into situations where they had paid the exteme penalty. He hoped that he was not looking at a future example of this through his binoculars' lenses.

Charlie was beyond the stage of deluding himself. He felt that John would come through today's test all right but that would lead to another and another. Would he ever be satisfied? Could it ever end peacefully for him? Realising that there was nobody who could direct John from his close way, Charlie chased these pessimistic thoughts from his head and watched closely as the lone figure set out on the second pitch.

Unaware of the watching lenses and the worrying thoughts, John continued on his way. The care with which he had climbed a difficult roof below told him that his form was good. His upward movements began to show confidence—not the over-confidence which traps many, but application of the knowledge of his ability. Stopping occasionally for rests he climbed the two remaining pitches in an hour until he was sitting at the high point of his previous attempts, breathing deeply to dissipate the tension but feeling very good indeed. The unknown was still to come but now he could take out some of the straight tension of the ascent by putting on the rope and giving himself an auto belay.

Charlie, seeing him start to place a series of belay pitons on the ledge, relaxed a little too. At least there was now some possibility of a fall being held. He also recognised the fact that he was witnessing a brilliant performance. John was obviously climbing very difficult rock and there was no doubt that he was totally attuned to the environment. Any worries Charlie might have had about this being an angry gesture at George's defection were dispersed. There could be one reason why John was up there and that was because he wanted to be there and was enjoying himself. But despite his success so far there was no cause for total rejoicing. The rope length above the tiny ledge where John was arranging equipment looked like the key to the climb.

Weaving in and out through the covering lichen, a thin crack ran into a double series of roofs, but unlike the roof he had climbed lower down these ones had no large cracks cutting through to make life easier. There were cracks, but they were as thin as the wall below, and non-continuous. John was obviously in for some difficult artificial climbing, placing one piton after another, standing in slings. It was the other side of rock climbing, slow laborious work compared with the dance of free climbing.

Munching chocolate, John sat cross-legged, putting the material slung around his body into order. He had a full selection of about thirty pitons, the largest being four inches wide and going down through nearly every shape and size to a couple of the American-named RURPs—realised ultimate reality pitons—literally the size of a postage stamp and made for use in extremely thin, shallow cracks. He arranged everything in descending order of size on a sling around his body so that he could select a piton by feel if necessary. Sometimes you get into positions where even turning your head is very precarious. On the other side he slung some forty karabiners or snap links.

Progress in artificial as opposed to free climbing is made by hammering in a piton, attaching a karabiner to the eye of the piton, and snapping a sling with three loops into the karabiner. You stand in the lowest loop, climb to the highest, and repeat the procedure. John was also going to use the auto-belay system: attached by slings to his harness he had two jumar clamps which he in turn attached to the rope, one above and one below the highest piton so that if the piton he was hanging from pulled, he would only have a normal leader fall. The trouble with this method was that the jumar clamps were not built to take long falls; if a series of pitons pulled out he was in danger of falling right to the end of the rope where the clamp would have too much of a shock load placed on it. This did not bear contemplating, for it meant a potential three-hundred-foot jump when it was doubtful if anything would hold: belay, pitons, rope, harness, body or bones. Although he was giving himself the maximum protection possible, John was by no means safe.

Checking the equipment, he examined himself too. Did he want to go on? Turning back was still easy, a matter of a mere three abseils. But his resolve was still very strong: his way out was upwards not downwards. He felt physically and mentally in very good shape as he stood up and started to place the first piton above the ledge. Straightaway the angle began to assert itself. He was pushed backwards and the placement was awkward. Selecting a knife blade piton about two inches long, he drove it in as far as it would go. About half way in, it reached the bottom of the shallow crack. He tied it off, winding a short length of string round the blade closest to the rock to reduce the leverage, clipped in an aid sling and tentatively stood up. Fine: it held. He climbed up the rungs of his aid slings until he could reach at full stretch and place another pin. He had to put six of these knife blades in a row, and, while they withstood his weight none of them would have held a fall. Standing on the sixth, John was distinctly worried. Falling now would have the effect of undoing a zip fastener. He wondered how many more of these placements he could safely justify before the risks were too great. He was placing the pitons as well as possible but his dependence on the mechanical process was total; his physical or mental climbing skill were irrelevant, and it was alien to his way of thinking. But he had no alternative. It was his only way—even retreating down that precarious ladder would not be easy, for pitons often slacken after you have passed.

He was right under the roofs, alone with these uneasy thoughts, when suddenly he blinked. He could hardly believe his eyes. Where his thin crack line joined the roof there was a short horizontal fault about half an inch wide, the best possible piton placement. Not hesitating for a second, he smoothly felt for an angle piton, banged it in to the hilt, clipped everything into it and let out a huge gasp as he relaxed. It was like an oasis in a desert: this one he could fall on and it would hold.

Swinging gently, he contemplated the roof. It was fairly short, coming out horizontally for five feet. Then there was a short vertical wall and another roof of similar dimensions. Reckoning that the pitons on the horizontal section of roof would be very poor, John decided to attach a long doubled sling to the good piton as an extra precaution in case one of them pulled out.

Leaning back horizontally, he selected the shortest of his knife blades and drove it straight in under the roof. About half way in it gave a dull sound and hit bottom. Resisting the futile temptation to hammer away further, John tapped it sideways. It gave a tight ringing sound, seemed to be okay. There was no way of tying off this pin: any pull would be straight down—and out. Clipping in an aid sling he tentatively stretched out and, still holding his good pin with one hand, put a foot in the sling. Slowly he eased his weight out on to it; still it held. Eventally he made the slow transfer of the other aid sling and then put his full weight on to the winking straining piece of metal. If it pulls, he thought grimly, it'll smash me straight in the face.

The next placement would bring him round the first roof and on to the vertical section beneath the second, where he hoped there would be a placement as good as that under the first roof. Stretched out horizontally under the roof, John could barely see the crack continuing round the tip. It broadened slightly but the rock was very compact and its cracks still shallow. No hope of swinging round on to something really good: it would be a long slow easing up process over again. Intent on solving the problem of the few feet of rock immediately in front of his eyes, John was ignorant of his spectacular position. Beneath his groping fingers there was nothing but four hundred feet of air to the ground below. The angle was so extreme that he could not see the pitches which he had already climbed, even if he had considered looking.

If John was unaware of his position Charlie certainly was not. No longer lounging in the sun, he was riveted to his binoculars. Seeing the tentative movements he was aware that the climbing had become very hard. And the position was sensational. The tiny red crash-helmeted figure hung alone in the great upthrust of the white wall.

Trying to put as little strain as possible on the knife blade, John stretched his hand round the edge of the roof. Unable to see the exact size of the crack, he probed it with his fingers and selected a short angle piton. He could not let go with one hand to tap it with the other. Feeling awkward and out of balance, he tried some different positions but nothing worked. He could see round the tip but could not pull up enough to get a good look at the crack. He was in an extremely difficult position, stretched out horizontally beneath the roof with his left hand round the tip, holding the piton, and his right trying to tap it in with a hammer. He gave it a few sharp blows by manipulating his wrist sharply but then came the sound he was dreading: the dull thump that meant it had reached the bottom of the crack. He could drive it no further though it had only gone in a very short distance. Often when this happens inexperienced climbers are tempted to hammer more and more, but all this does is loosen what precarious grip the piton already has and make it useless. Too wise to make this mistake, John let his hammer swing from its sling, selected a short tie-off loop and placed it on the piton right next to the rock.

Knowing it was potentially a bad one, he attached a safety sling to his aid sling before clipping it on to the reluctant pin so that he would not lose it if the piton came out. Checking his safety sling to the start of the roof, he gave the pin above a long slow pull. It did not move. Transferring a foot to the loop, he pulled cautiously round the edge. Still the pin held.

First he saw the piton. And he did not like it at all. The eye and four inches of metal were profiled against the sky, meaning that only an inch or so was bearing his weight. Forcing himself to look away he glanced up the cliff. Up there it was better, for a continuous fault line ran from above the placement right out to the edge of the outer lip of the second roof. If this one held, he could get up the rest. Carefully, he reached back under the roof for another aid sling, hardly daring even to breathe.

Charlie, with his binoculars riveted on the piton and John's slow movements, did not breathe at all. Suddenly there was nothing in his sights. Swearing violently and fearfully he wrenched them down, just in time to see John jerk in a wild tangled heap into inactivity a merciful six feet beneath the good pin. For a few seconds John knew nothing. His safety sling had stopped the fall when the bad pin came out but the jerk had smashed him face first against the rock. The front of his helmet had taken the brunt of the blow but the scraping of the rock had opened cuts which were bleeding into his eyes. Slowly he pulled back into consciousness, wondering where he was. Wiping his eyes, his first reaction was to shout to George that he seemed to be okay. Then the next step of realisation: there was no George. Finding that all his limbs worked he concentrated on cleaning his eyes and began slowly to take stock of the situation. True he was alone, and he had taken a fall, but his precautions had worked. Except for a few bruises he was all right. Should he go down? No, that would be more dangerous than trying to continue. A piton had pulled but his back up had been good. He could justifiably try again. Slowly he collected the jumbled mass of equipment that was hanging loose around him and moved up on his jumars to the good piton to deliberate his position.

Both the top pin and the knife blade under the roof had pulled before the good angle had brought him up tight. Thanks to his safety precautions, he had not lost any equipment. Tying a silk scarf round his forehead to stem the blood from the cuts, he methodically began to rearrange the gear.

Down below, Charlie's first reaction had been to rush towards the cliff. Realising the futility of this, he took hold of his whirling thoughts, trained the binoculars on the slumped figure and watched the slow movements of reorientation. He wanted to shout, "Come down son, you've tried your best, don't push your luck, wait for a partner," but he had not lived twenty-five years in the mountains for nothing. He knew this was only an automatic trigger response, the archetypal crowd reaction from his unconscious. With a long sigh he settled down to watch again knowing that the struggle was going to continue.

Sometimes you get irrational feelings about whether something is going to be good or bad. Despite his fall John felt more optimistic about the climbing than he had done before. Replacing the knife blade was easy, and for the bad placement he decided to use a shorter thicker pin. This time it went in up to the hilt and almost before he knew what he had done, he was past the bad part and banging in two extremely solid pins beneath the next roof. He had to remove the pitons below but with a good upper anchor it was no trouble to take them out on the way down, swing way out into space and jumar back up to his high point.

To Charlie, the little figure penduluming and swinging on the rope looked sensational against the awe-inspiring mass of rock. John was climbing smoothly and easily and on the good crack continuation he was suddenly a pitoning machine as he hammered out over the roof and into the dazzling freedom of mere verticality above. Expecting blank walls he was surprised to see that there were plenty of holds. After he had depitoned the last roof stretch he decided to put away the rope and free solo. It was easier above but when you have done something extremely hard you tend to relax when easier ground arrives, and this is when accidents happen. Aware of the danger, John moved onto the rock above with all his normal concentration. It was still very severe climbing but the pleasure of being able to move freely after the confinement of the roof below, combined with his magnificent natural ability, seemed to make him flow upwards. Minutes later he was sitting at the top of the cliff barely aware that he had completed the hardest climb in Scotland alone.

In his hideaway Charlie quickly gathered up the tripod, binoculars and the couple of cans of beer he had packed in case of celebration. Already he could see a figure running down the scree slopes in obvious elation. John had wasted no time at the top and after arranging his ropes and ironmongery had quickly stuffed them in his sac and started down. Time had passed quickly: it was late afternoon and the short September day was beginning to slip away into dull greens and purples. After the harshness of the rock scenery and the imprisoning confinement of his concentration the shadow of the Glen below seemed soft and unusually beautiful. Now that relaxation was permitted he could open his mind and let the impressions whirl. Later there would be analysis and future things to contemplate but meanwhile he could drift in the pleasant limbo that comes after hard physical and mental exercise.

Running down the path, he saw a lone figure crossing the river and starting up the path. He wondered who it could be at that time of day. Fifteen minutes later he ground to a stop, breathing hard, beside a smiling Charlie.

"Well done, lad, but you'd better learn to place better pitons or I'd have had to drink this myself," he said, passing a can of beer to John.

Momentarily surprised, but seeing the binoculars in the pack, John realised that he had not been as alone as he thought. Moved by this gesture of Charlie's he replied in the same bantering tone: "Been playing Peeping Tom again eh? Christ, it's impossible to find any peace in Glencoe these days."

"Privilege of old age. How was it?"

Sinking down into the heather with a can of beer John told him the story of the day's climb. Charlie was silent, knowing he was getting the true story while John's mind had still not come down totally. Later accounts would be more polished and toned down. In the dying light of a beautiful day, he listened to the revelations of a troubled mind temporarily at ease, satisfied for a brief moment. The story was intriguing: it had obviously been a tremendous experience but as the sun dropped down and John came to the end of his story he had a pang of sadness at the knowledge that it would not be enough. John would have to continue and a continuance at that level could only have its logical conclusion one day.

Charlie had never been afraid of death but he had never gone looking for it like a knight of the round table searching for the Holy Grail. It was always present but in his mountaineering he had always been careful to avoid violent confrontations. He felt that having been granted a period of living, which he enjoyed, it was reasonable to take precautions against terminating it suddenly. He knew nothing about death; who did, except the dead? But since the experience would eventually come to him whether he liked it or not, he preferred to live his life appreciating it to the full and not seeking to hasten the inevitable.

John's attitude gave him a lot to think about, for while John was certainly no more afraid of death than Charlie he appeared to have a puzzling disregard for life itself. It seemed to Charlie that the whole of John's life was spent in formulating challenges which would bring him as close to death as possible; when he successfully avoided it, he was only content until the time he could launch into a greater and closer struggle. Having been a mountaineer for so many years Charlie could appreciate that John was getting an awful lot out of what he was doing but his experience seemed almost narrow in its very concentration. Did he realise how many beautiful things he was missing in life? Charlie doubted it. Fanaticism is all-consuming but blinkered, and John was a fanatic albeit a nice one. But Charlie knew well enough not to press his opinions on others, especially in theoretical matters where he wasn't quite sure of himself. His thoughts would remain unvoiced. He liked John; he admired his brilliant progress in the world of mountaineering, and that was that. Instead, as the evening gloom settled on the Glen, Charlie said "Would you like to have a meal at my place? Hopefully the girls should be down by now. I've got a leg of lamb and some nice red you might be interested in."

"Couldn't think of a better way of finishing off the day," John said warmly. "Thanks, Charlie, see you at the house."

CHAPTER 4

CHARLIE

Tailing Charlie slowly John realised how hungry he was as the thought of good food and wine began to displace the day's climb in his thoughts. Like many middle-aged bachelors who had travelled a lot and were used to looking after themselves, Charlie was a good cook and loved his wines. In a dark little cave beneath the cottage he kept a small but choice selection. True to character Charlie did not go in for well-established classics or expensive Chateau bottled wine, preferring to scout around the young wines from the less well-known areas and countries. Despite many mistakes he had become an expert on the wines of Switzerland, Italy, Greece and Yugoslavia, many of which should be drunk young and do not take to lurking around in musty cellars for years.

Pulling in to the cottage, they saw that the two girls were sitting outside drinking tea, looking pleased with themselves. Anxious looks passed over their faces as they saw Charlie's car alone, but when the low-revving Honda pulled out from behind and rolled to a stop in front of them they broke into wide smiles. Before they could ask the inevitable question, Charlie waved his thumb in the air and disappeared into the house, leaving John in sudden danger of suffocation as he was enveloped by two healthy and happy females.

"You got up?" they cried simultaneously.

John disengaged himself and, putting an arm around each, led them back to the bench where they had been sitting.

"Of course. What do you expect? And how about the women's lib team?"

"What do you expect," said Cathy, coming back fast. "We did Big Top. It's a fabulous route."

"Jesus Christ. I'd better watch out. That sounds like competition on the horizon." But John was impressed by the girls' performance. "Who led the overhang?"

– 47 –

Cathy jerked a thumb at Judy. "Junior here. Bounced over out of sight before I had time to see what was happening."

Judy smiled and stayed silent. It had been a good effort by the girls. Big Top had been done in the early 'sixties by the late great Robin Smith, one of the most talented climbers ever to come out of Scotland, and while not desperately difficult in a technical sense it had some moves which were bold, exposed and committing, like the overhang that John had asked about.

Charlie reappeared out of the house with a tray and some cans of chilled beer. Laying it on the table, he said: "Here, get into this and you can get the day's news out of your system while I make supper."

Judy broke in: "What can we do, Charlie?"

He waved the offer away. "I'm much more at home alone in my kitchen and besides I've done nothing but lie in the heather all day. Just relax. You can wash up later."

Realising that this was the final word, the two girls and John settled down, chatting quietly in the soft night while Charlie went to work, whistling to himself in the kitchen. The conversation was non-specific and vague as they relaxed thoughtfully after the day's efforts. They touched briefly on winter climbing in the Alps. With everything crowded in summer and some of the greater challenges left in Europe to be done, it was the growing sport. John and George had talked seriously about going out in January but that project would now have to be scrapped. There would be time to reconsider the matter in the next few months as the rock climbing season was drawing to a close: October and November are traditional low-key months in Scottish climbing and most people content themselves with wandering on the hill and climbing boulder problems.

The low murmur of their voices was broken by a cheerful shout from the kitchen. "O.K., come and get it."

They needed no second prompting. Swallowing the last of the beer they trooped into the small dining room which reflected Charlie's quiet good taste: a low ceiling with genuine old wood beams, walls covered with black and white mountain prints, a few well-used armchairs and, the central attraction, a rough wood table set for four.

"What's the wine special tonight then, Charlie?" John peered at the two bottles labelled 'Monseigneur' on the table. "My, that's a grand title."

"Aye and it's a grand wine," replied Charlie pouring it out. "Tell me what you think of it. Cheers."

"Cheers, Charlie," they chorused, and drank while Charlie watched them carefully over the top of the wine glasses. This was one of his favourites and he wanted to see the effect on young, still unformed palates. He also knew that if they did not like it they would tell him in no uncertain manner.

"Aye, not bad," murmured John, setting his glass down.

Cathy broke in spluttering: "What do you mean you bloody dour Scot, 'not bad'? It's fabulous. How did you find out about this one, Charlie?"

With a grin of happy memory, Charlie described his encounter with the wine.

"A few years ago, I'd done a climb on the Dents du Midi, above Martigny, with a Swiss friend and we were driving back to Lausanne when he suggested a dinner at Bex. It's a small village right under the Dents du Midi: we could contemplate our day's efforts out of the dining-room window. It was late September, a beautiful time of year and also the hunting season in Switzerland. We had saddle of venison and this wine which comes from the vineyards of Aigle, a small town close by. I've been addicted to it ever since, but it's harder to get in this country than a Chateau Lafitte. The Swiss export hardly any of their wines: they drink most of the good ones themselves. Fortunately, I know a couple of Swiss air hostesses and in exchange for the odd meal on one of their London stopovers, they bring me bottles of my Swiss favourites, and as I'm fairly often in London I can usually keep ahead of the score that way."

The others smiled as Charlie started to carve the lamb. Charlie's contacts were legendary. If you wanted something from, or some information about, any of the countries he had travelled in, he always knew someone or had a contact. Hence his house in Glencoe was seldom empty. On a favour-for-favour basis, his contacts were always invited to sample Highland hospitality and many did, from ambassadors to hitchhikers. The evenings were often gay and hectic, but this one was different. Replete with food and wine, they sat languidly sipping coffee and listening to Charlie talk about some of his expeditions.

Again the talk turned easily to winter climbing in the Alps, but this time John, confronted with the full impact of George's defection, found the subject difficult. Judy, watching him, saw his face close up, while Charlie looked at first puzzled, then concerned and finally rather pleased as something evidently occurred to him. Judy wondered what he was up to.

Whatever his train of thought, it was interrupted by the purr of the telephone. As he went to answer it, the girls got up silently and started to move the debris of the meal towards the kitchen. A few minutes later Charlie wandered back in.

"It was Donnie, at the Hotel. His father is seriously ill in Glasgow and he's going to have to drive down tonight. He asked if I'd take charge for a couple of days. Are you coming down or do you want to stay here? There's plenty of drink in the house."

"Thanks, Charlie," replied John, "but I think I'll come down to the pub. Got to catch up with the day's news, you know. If you don't mind though, I'll drive down in the car. I don't want to take the bike; could be a heavy night."

"Sure, I'll just change and if you can get those women out of the kitchen we'll be off."

The two girls needed no persuading and soon they were driving down the narrow track towards the hotel.

CHAPTER 5

PUNCH-UP AT THE CLACHAIG

The fickle West Highland weather was playing games again. When they had been sitting outside before dinner it had been a fine, soft starlit night but only two hours later the stars were veiled and black clouds were moving fast over Loch Leven. Glencoe is very close to the sea and suffers from rapid weather changes, which any West Highland fisherman will tell you about at length and in return for a glass of whisky.

"Aye," Charlie broke the silence as the lights of the hotel came in sight and they were already passing parked cars, way outside the car park, "Donnie certainly picks the nights to go away. It looks as if it's going to be like Glasgow fair holiday in there."

This reference was to the annual two weeks holiday, in July, of most working men from Glasgow, when a large majority do their best to drink the West Coast pubs out of beer. John nodded agreement.

"The weather's going to be bad tomorrow, so everyone'll be getting blasted. I wish you luck; you might have to throw a few people out tonight."

Scotsmen when drinking heavily often have a belligerent streak and even amongst the close-knit climbing community fights were by no means a rarity.

They pulled around into the private car park behind the hotel as Charlie said: "See you after closing time. I think we'll get rid of everyone on time tonight. There's a dance in the village."

In the Clachaig Inn, there was no difference between lounge and public bar. Just one big room, but it did not seem so big as John and the girls tried to force their way into it. It seemed to be bursting at the seams with red-faced, perspiring climbers clutching pints of beer and talking at the tops of their voices.

John kept returning greetings as he tried to reach the bar

while the girls were ducking familiar hands that kept reaching out from the crowd.

Catching sight of Mark Jones the Englishman, who was just about to get an order, John gave him a shout: "Hey, Mark, can you get me three pints, it'll save me waiting 'till closing time."

"Hi Johnny." Mark yelled back. "I'll even buy them for you. That was a nice route of yours that we did today. Tom's over in the corner with some of your Edinburgh mates; we've got a table, you can probably squeeze in there. . . Can you grab some of these beers and take them over?"

A tray full of pints came over several wary heads into John's hands. Seeing his friends in the corner John started what should have been a perilous journey but a passage miraculously appeared through the bodies. Laughing to himself, he muttered in Judy's ear: "Christ, they have no respect for man, woman, authority or beast but show them a pint of beer and they'll go out of their way to be nice to it."

He plumped the tray on the table to cries of: "Well now, look who's here?" and they settled into a session of climbing gossip. There were lots of surprised faces when the news of John's solo climb got around. There were perhaps a dozen climbers around the table, the majority very good, and in their faces Judy's watchful eyes picked up a variety of reactions. Some were quite different from the outwardly-voiced congratulations for, as well as genuine respect, they showed the fear, awe, envy and resignation typical of people in varying forms of competition who are suddenly faced with the realisation that someone nearby is in a slightly different and better class than they. But they listened quietly enough as John gave a brief summation of the difficulties he had found, knowing this to be easier than answering a barrage of different questions.

A few of them were already thinking of the second ascent, he realised, for it is one of the strange phenomena of climbing that there are always more people to repeat things than there are to do first ascents. It continually baffled John, with his love for delving into the unknown, but it was true. Perhaps it was a characteristic of the prevalent Twentieth century life pattern where the majority seemed to need certainty and security in their way of living. Even George fitted into that pattern, he thought painfully, remembering his partner for the first time since the climb. Watching the faces around him as he finished talking he suddenly felt alien, just as alone as he had been on the rocks of Aonach Dubh.

And then he felt two eyes boring into his innermost thoughts. Catching Judy's glance he winked, thinking: "This one bears watching—she knows exactly what's going on." He turned to talk to her when a sudden commotion at the bar caused the whole room to break off their conversations.

A heavy character, dressed in a black leather jacket, even in the heat of the bar, was arguing with one of the barmen.

"Oh-oh, here comes trouble," muttered John, with the wisdom of experience.

The run up to Fort William from Glasgow was a favourite with the motorcycle gangs from Glasgow. The majority, fortunately, confined their activities to the section along Loch Lomond side but occasionally a group would come further afield. Apart from playing with motorcycles, their activities consisted of getting drunk and picking fights. The fights were usually unequal in number, with the majority on their side, and it was seldom a question of going outside and settling it with fists. More usually bottles, broken glass and boots sent their unfortunate victims to hospital. This champion was complaining about having to wait for a drink, while the barman was explaining that everyone was in the same boat, that it was a particularly busy night and that if he ordered it would speed up the proceedings.

A small climber standing beside him said jokingly: "C'mon Jimmy, get yer order in. We're all dying of thirst."

The biker turned on him, snarling: "What's it go to do with you anyway?" grabbed the small man by the lapels, butted him savagely between the eyes and, as he dropped, kicked him in the ribs with a heavy leather riding boot.

The bar hushed. Silently four other leather-clad figures slid in behind the first, bottles and chains appearing in their hands. The figure on the floor was unconscious and bleeding heavily.

"We'd better get out of here, Tam," muttered one of the gang.

Tam turned to the ring of silent faces challengingly. "We're going, but if anyone else wants a dose of the same they're welcome." Then he sneered: "Let's go. There's no action here."

How sadly he had underestimated the action he never found out until the next morning. The gang had been too busy with the people around them to notice about a dozen climbers slipping out of the side doors and making their way towards the front entrance. All the climbers' rowdy arguments had stopped as the gang, an alien element, threatened the happy system of their little world. Many of them were from rough backgrounds and knew all about gang wars and street fighting. Many had taken to the mountains to escape from that kind of environment, but they had not forgotten the lessons they had learned. As well as a common love for the hills, they had a hatred of unnecessary violence.

Charlie, who had been watching all the movements from a room beside the bar, knew exactly what was happening. He could have called the police but with the gang in its present mood the sergeant and his constable would have been badly beaten up if they had tried to make an arrest. The bikers did not care if they went to prison: having kicked two policemen unconscious would give them more kudos with other gang members when they came out.

As the gang pushed open the doors into the yard, they relaxed and started joking at the one who had started the fight. "That was all right, Tam, but ye finished the action too fast. There was nothing left for us."

A quiet voice from the shadows outside silenced their noisy chatter.

"There's plenty left, you cowardly fuckers!" A small figure launched itself from the gloom, planting a climbing boot with devastating accuracy between Tam's legs.

Howling, he dropped into an agonized crouch, only to be met by an incoming knee which smashed his nose. As he blindly groped at the source of this new pain a second kick in the groin sent him into a dimension of agony he had never known. He was not unconscious, but his assailant, standing back watching him weeping and grovelling in the mud, had not wanted to be so merciful.

It had happened so quickly that the rest of the gang had

not had time to think. Like street animals, they turned together on the small figure of Willie Holt, bicycle chains
appearing in their hands. But that was their second mistake.
Intent on Willie, they were unaware of a second group that
poured out of the shadows and started attacking in the same
fashion. It was a massacre. Within minutes there were five
other leather-clad figures in varying states of unconsciousness
or extremely painful wakefulness lying in the yard. Willie Holt
left them surrounded by the watchful climbers and, pushing
open the door, shouted inside: "O.K. Charlie, you can call
Sergeant McNab. I think he's got some guests for tonight. Er
— and maybe you'd better get an ambulance as well."

The small climber who had been attacked was sitting in a
deep chair surrounded by a sympathetic crowd, having his face
bathed by one of the barmaids.

"Are you all right, Tony?"

"Aye Willie, he got me on the side of the face. He missed
my nose but he's loosened a few teeth. Ah feel as if ma brain's
loose but otherwise ah'm O.K. Did ye get him?"

"Aye. He'll no be troublin' anybody for a while."

The bar was starting to settle when a thick-set red-faced
police sergeant walked in. Seeing Willie he stopped: "Oh, it's
you, Holt. Been doing me out of a job again?"

Willie grinned: "Aye, Sergeant. I wish these motorcycle
gangs would stop fightin' each other. And they can't even
hold their drink. I was just takin' a turn outside with my girl
friend when they started fighting amongst themselves and as I
didn't want to see Donnie's yard destroyed I asked Charlie to
give you a ring."

A brief smile crossed the Sergeant's face. "It's good to have
a public-spirited crowd, makes life easier." He turned to Tony.
"Well, Tony, been falling off mountains again?"

With the nearest he could manage to a grin, Tony said:
"Aye, Sergeant, the Glencoe rocks are hard."

"Set these two up with whatever they want," McNab
ordered Charlie "and the same goes for my special constables
outside. I'd better go and look after my guests. I think I'll be
busy until midnight but I'll come back to see you're not staying open too late."

Charlie laughed as the Sergeant walked out of the door, for

this amounted to carte blanche to stay open until twelve o'clock under the principle that what the law doesn't want to see, it doesn't want to know about. As the police van pulled off into the night, the climbers who had been outside came milling into the bar to find their beers already lined up on the counter.

Incidents of this kind, while relatively unusual, had happened before. When disturbed, the climbers always closed their ranks to protect their home territory. Despite the diversity of their society, it was bound together by their common love of the mountains. Both the outdoor and indoor aspects of their weekend gatherings were precious to them and they would even fight to preserve them, for if word got around that climbers were soft touches then they would be invaded by people like those they had just disposed of. The typical motorbike gang members' enjoyment was predatory, derived from tormenting others. There was very little pleasure in their lives unless of the vicious animal kind and they could not bear to see others enjoying themselves. Outward happiness and laughter seemed to jog the viciousness in them like a hair trigger.

Sociologists might say that if one regarded their backgrounds this kind of thing was understandable and that they needed help, a valid point of view if they could be talked to individually, but in the bar environment things were different. How do you offer help to a pack of snarling animals, inflamed by alcohol, who are turning to attack? In this situation jungle law holds: force must be met with force. People like Willie Holt and his friends came from similar backgrounds to the gangs, the mean tenements and streets of the slum areas of Glasgow. By sheer willpower they had fought their way out of the depressing, mind-destroying environment. Introduced to mountains and sports by altruistic youth leaders, they had found another world, and once having escaped, they vowed never to return to the streets of their childhood. Because they knew what they could fall back into, their will to get ahead in the normal world was immense. Willie, who had a successful contracting business, was a passionate weekend climber, having always retained a great love for the sport that was instrumental in his leaving his background behind.

But since he had run with the gangs until he was sixteen, then fought himself through an apprenticeship in the Clyde-side docks, he was a man it was unwise to tangle with when the going got tough. Others might have tried to talk to the gangs, but Willie and his like-minded mates knew that they regarded attempts to reason as a sign of cowardice.

The display of raw aggression produced a sudden reaction in John. The long, eventful day had eventually caught up with him. The conversation around seemed like a distant buzzing in his ears. Occasionally he reacted automatically to a question addressed to him, but was not taking any active part in the discussions and though he was usually interested in such sessions, he realised that tonight was not one of those times.

Leaning over to Judy, he said "I think I'll ask Charlie if I can stay at his place tonight. I don't feel like pitching the tent in this weather."

Charlie was his usual hospitable self. "Sure, John. In fact I think I'll stay up here tonight. There's quite a few guests and I'll probably have to get breakfast organised. Anyway, by the time I've watered the police after closing time it'll hardly be worthwhile going to bed. Take the van back and I'll give you a ring in the morning and you can pick me up. Somehow I don't think there'll be much climbing tomorrow."

"Thanks, Charlie, that's really nice of you. See you in the morning," John said, taking the proferred car keys. He found Judy at his elbow.

"I heard Charlie's offer; do you mind giving me another lift? I'm tired too and somehow I don't think Cathy will be coming back tonight. They're talking about taking a load of beer back to the Squirrel Club hut for a party and she's all for going."

Smiling, John replied: "Why surely Miss Scott," adding with a flash of reflective malice, "but it may not be quite like last night. I'm pretty weary."

Coming back fast Judy said: "What about those famous powers of recovery? Tomorrow's another day."

Seeing the innuendo, and liking it, John could feel once again the germs of something pleasant growing up between them. Laughing together they slipped out of the back door before the party people could start trying to change their minds.

Outside, it had turned into what is commonly known as a typical Glencoe night. Rain was slashing horizontally along the Glen and the car's wiper could barely cope with the rush of water.

"Not exactly a night for camping," remarked Judy as they pulled up outside the darkened cottage.

"Even worse for a bivouac. Let's hope there's no rescues in the Glen tonight," John replied, the mountains going through his head as usual.

This was not a facetious statement. There were many nights when a forlorn figure would stagger into the pub looking for help or Charlie's phone would ring in the midst of a good dinner and they would have to turn out into the night to look for a victim. Mountain rescue in Glencoe was voluntary. The official team, of which Charlie was leader comprised some of the more active residents of the Glen such as the police and shepherds, but Charlie invariably had a band of regular climbing visitors whom he called out to supply the technical expertise which the locals were lacking. This worked on a favour-for-favour basis. The climbers always went out to rescue one of their kind working on the assumption that if they got into trouble their fellows would do the same for them.

It was one of the reasons why the climbers had a good relationship with the local police, for there is nothing quite like working together on a rain-swept cliff at midnight looking for some shattered piece of humanity to bring people together. Often the only reward was a missed night's sleep and a free round of whisky at one of the local hotels.

"I think we're safe tonight," continued John, laughing. "Anyway the person who called that mob out of the bar tonight would have a lot to answer for. They're hardly capable of looking after themselves, far less anyone else."

There was still a glimmer of light from the fire and they sat on the rug drinking some coffee, chattering inconsequentially until they found they had gradually eased into a long relaxed session of love-making, the pleasure coursing gently through their already tired bodies. Sometime in the night John got up and found a blanket, but they stayed curled up happily on the sheepskin like the two primitives they really were, and for once, John did not think about mountains.

Judy woke first at around 8 a.m. From where she lay she could see that the rain had stopped, but dark grey clouds were still hanging low on the flanks of the Aonach Eagach ridge, across the valley. There was something almost womb-like in the feeling of lying warm and pleasant in this cosy room surveying the tormented world outside. Looking at John's sleeping figure she was aware that they were starting to become close but with her usual realism, she knew that even if the relationship developed she would still be 'Number Two' to the mountains. It did not trouble her. She knew that to have a good relationship with someone you must embrace all the facets of the other person's character without trying to exclude things. She felt that she could do that with John, and that it was time to make the break with Don. Their relationship had deteriorated to the point where they were staggering along on old memories and achieving nothing fresh. For a time, she had been ready to finish it but its very security had made her lazy, although she did not want the marriage that Don, she felt, would eventually suggest. There were too many things to do now that she was near the end of her studies. . .

Whatever happened, she was glad of the weekend that had passed: talking, lovemaking and climbing had fused into a warm memory. She smiled and slipped quietly from under the blanket so that John woke slowly to soft piano music and the smell of coffee. Recognising Schumann's 'Song of dawn', he closed his eyes and let the peace of the music run through his relaxed mind. Judy could not have chosen more sympathetically: this often under-rated work for piano, the last thing that the composer wrote before his genius crossed the thin edge into insanity, was one of his favourite pieces.

Slipping into a sweater and jeans, he padded to the window to survey the weather. Decisive as ever, he dismissed climbing. After yesterday's effort and before the long Alpine season, it was time for some relaxation, for though his dedication towards the mountains was total, he realised the necessity of a complete break occasionally, purely to recharge body and mind.

New thoughts in his head, he wandered into the kitchen.

Putting his arms round her from behind, he could feel the firm lithe body under the old dressing-gown of Charlie's that she was wearing. Repressing other thoughts, he introduced the day in facetious fashion. "You don't seem to be carrying much weight these days despite the breakfasts you cook."

Pushing him away with a grin, Judy went into the attack: "You don't exactly look like an advert for gourmet cooking yourself. Too many bivouac meals. Maybe a course of my cooking would do us both good. I'm pretty reasonable at it. I've been semi-domesticated for three years."

In old-fashioned society this rather blatant remark would have been frowned upon. But in the free-thinking climbing society woman approaching man was quite a normal thing. They were both on equal terms and the female had as much right to declare her intentions as the male.

"Right on both points, girl. I've been thinking. The summer season's pretty well over. I've got to go back to Edinburgh for a week or so to finish some work and then I was thinking of heading down towards the Lake District for a couple of weeks—you know, usual end-of-season stuff, reading, walking a lot, thinking about projects and getting my mind back into shape for looking at some philosophy next term. Point is, the bike takes two, so does the tent, and I think we could get on together. What do you think?"

Hiding her pleasure in a flurry of turning sausages and eggs, Judy said briefly: "Done. You've got a mate, providing we can go back through Glasgow so I can pick up some more gear . . . and I might have to make one or two touchy 'phone calls from Edinburgh."

"That's O.K.," said John pensively, realising she was thinking of Don's reactions. "I'll have to do the same myself."

In both of their statements they unconsciously displayed the positive attitude of upper level climbing. Both realised their mutual attraction, and both wanted to explore it. To do it they were prepared to cut through any preventative barriers. These included what seemed to their present way of thinking relationships of convenience. Don and Pat must not stand in their way. With the main decisions made, John left Judy to clean up the cottage while he drove back to the hotel. He found a rather dishevelled Charlie in the kitchen drinking coffee with the staff.

"Hard night, Charlie?"

Regarding him with slightly bloodshot eyes, Charlie grunted: "What are you looking so bloody cheerful about? I didn't get rid of the Sergeant until six-thirty this morning and most of the guests stayed up as well. We've only had three for breakfast, but I definitely feel in need of freshening up."

"You certainly look it," commented the cook. "If you don't want to frighten the guests you'd better go home for a couple of hours."

Laughing, John and Charlie drove back to the cottage to find Judy reading quietly, a fresh pot of coffee on the stove. "Thought you'd need that," she said, looking him up and down, "and I wasn't too far wrong, either. Tell us about it then. . ."

By the time John had the packs strapped on the bike ready to go the sun was filtering weakly through the cloud and the steam rising from the roads hinted it could even be a pleasant ride down.

Judy kissed Charlie: "Thanks a million, love, see you soon."

John gave him a playful punch on the shoulder. "See you at the start of winter and many thanks."

Charlie roused himself from the doze he was falling into. "Aye, O.K. Don't do anything I wouldn't do."

"Well, that gives us a lot of license."

The Honda engine ticked over easily and soon they were winding through the Glen admiring the watery sun playing on the black slime that had been yesterday's dry cliffs. By 5 p.m. they were pulling up outside John's small flat in the Fountainbridge district of Edinburgh, close to the University.

They were still there nine days later when the telegram came.

"Who the hell would send me a telegram?" John muttered as he opened the envelope.

As he glanced at the contents, an expression of surprise came over his face. It read simply: "If interested in Jorasses this winter, call Leysin. McDonald."

"Well, well," he said, handing the form to Judy. "I didn't expect that."

Jack McDonald was in his mid-thirties and acknowledged as one of the best mountaineers in the world. Having done nearly all the major European climbs he had turned his attention brilliantly to the Himalayas and had been one of the first to climb major big peaks by difficult faces. With a Swiss mother and American father, he had dual nationality and was now based in Leysin, Switzerland making a good living as a free-lance guide and photographer.

John had met him two years before in Chamonix, visited his chalet in Leysin and done a few local climbs with him. They had got on well together and though they had talked about the perennial last great problems as climbers always do, McDonald had never given a hint of forming a team. He usually climbed with a chosen few friends and seemed not to want to form new climbing partnerships.

With a new light in his eyes, John answered Judy's questioning gaze: "I don't need to tell you the answer. This is a gift from heaven. I was wondering what to do about the winter now that George has packed in and here it is: one of the best objectives in the Alps with one of the best climbers. I'm going to call Jack straight away."

Judy smiled at the happiness and enthusiasm shining in his eyes and went off to have a shower as John started to dial Switzerland.

CHAPTER 6

LEYSIN

The sun, swinging low over Lac Leman, looked as if it were going to disappear for ever into the thick bank of cold weather cloud that usually hides the Swiss valleys in late autumn. The figure resting easily on skis on a hillside six thousand feet above scarcely noticed what for the majority of people would have been an impressive sight. He glanced leftwards across the Dents du Midi, but did not pause to examine their difficult-looking faces, for he knew them to be a false front: great to look at but nothing behind, a poor climber's mountain. Instead, he looked beyond, to Mont Blanc and the Chamonix satellites, which were just changing into their late autumn colours. If he had swung his head around a full hundred and eighty degrees he would have had as fine a view of the Alps as one could find anywhere. Everything was out this day: leftwards from Chamonix, the Grand Combin, Dent Blanche and Matterhorn; then many lower peaks and the climax of the Eiger and Mönch on the extreme left. It was a view that Jack McDonald seldom failed to appreciate, just as he appreciated most views of mountains from Scotland through to the Himalayas. But today his thoughts were not on the peaks he could see but on the greatest north face in the Chamonix region which, from his viewpoint, was hidden by the bulk of the Aiguille Verte.

The Grandes Jorasses is, to non-climbers anyway, the least known of the great mountain triumvirate Eiger, Matterhorn and Jorasses, probably because it is the shyest and most retiring of the three. The other two stand proudly out in the open, dominating their neighbours, exhibiting themselves for anyone to see; but the Jorasses is hidden in a corner, surrounded by other peaks. And it is not one peak, but no less than six separate ones, giving a formidable sextuplet of steep north faces. Those on the Pointes Croz and Walker had been climbed after many attempts, retreats and epics in the 'thirties, and now there were routes on all six north walls. There had even been winter ascents on the Walker, Croz and Marguerita, but what was occupying Jack McDonald's thoughts so totally at the moment was the idea of a completely new route, in winter, on the unclimbed west flank of the Pointe Walker.

Of the six points, the Walker is not only the highest but also the most elegant. Its original line on the crest of the buttress, first climbed in 1938 by the Italians Cassin, Esposito and Tizzoni, is regarded as one of the finest, most exciting and aesthetically pleasing classic lines in the Alps. But on its west flank is another face which seems like the dark side of the Walker's character. Most people have parts of their minds which they try to hide or cover up because of the potential evil that lurks therein. It seems as though the Walker Spur were trying to do that to its forbidding west face. Completely different in looks and character from the fine rocky crest, the west face's ice fields, steep verglassed couloirs and overhanging headwall leading to the summit are all continuously swept by murderous stonefall. No-one had seriously contemplated climbing it. The great French climbers, Lachenal and Terray, once wandered across one of its upper ice fields, by mistake, in the cloud, on an ascent of the Walker Spur. Their description afterwards was brief and to the point: "a thoroughly nonrecommendable variant". But that was in summer; in winter the ice that plastered it froze the shattered rock into merciful stillness. A bold man, undeterred by the additional hazards of a winter ascent, could see that here was a major unclimbed face, one of the steadily decreasing few left in the Alps.

Jack, at thirty-five, was regarded as one of the best climbers around. Before moving on to the vast and difficult unclimbed faces in the Himalayas he had been totally involved in Alpine climbing, and as he gained more and more experience he tended to swing to the winter side of it. Amongst many other important ascents he had climbed both the North faces of the Eiger and Matterhorn in winter, but he had never made a winter attempt on any of the Jorasses routes.

The previous autumn, while waiting for a client in the Couvercle Hut and peering absent-mindedly at the Jorasses, he had slowly become aware of the huge gap between the Walker Spur and the Central Couloir which bounded the face on its right. After that he was no longer absent-minded. His sharp eye had quickly picked out a line going pretty well straight up the centre of the wall. He knew that there were climbers interested in the Central Couloir in winter, which he had always regarded as an indefinite and scrappy line. But he had never overheard a mention of the west face of the Pointe Walker, and since climbers talk all the time about possible new routes he certainly would have been aware of rumours of any attempt. Later he had done a lot of research and examination of photographs and they had all pointed to one conclusion: a potential route existed, and a good one.

After that there were only two things to do as far as he was concerned, pick the time and choose a partner. The first was relatively straightforward. It would have to be in winter as he had seen and heard about the holocaust in the Central Colouir area in summer. On a bivouac on a summer ascent of the Walker Spur he had been kept awake by the constant rattle of falling rocks to his right in the couloir—and that was at night, everything was supposed to be frozen!

Jack had pushed himself close to the limit in desperate situations many times during his career but one thing that was missing in his mental make-up was any form of suicidal tendency, despite the popular opinions to the contrary. So winter it would have to be.

Driving his skis upwards in the twilight, for he still had one summit left to do on his training round of the Leysin peaks, he reflected on his choice of partner.

For most of his climbing career Jack had restricted his partners to a circle of close friends on his major ascents. Naturally he climbed with many strangers during the course of his guiding but he regarded this as another side of mountaineering, more concerned with care and safety than moving into the realms of the unknown.

He was not a solo climber, either by nature or inclination, preferring to share the end of a hard day with a companion. Climbing is always lonely for the person doing the leading, as Jack mostly did, and it lessens the tension and strain to have someone with you on a belay or a bivouac, especially a friend with whom you have shared many experiences.

But on reaching the age of thirty-five, having worked at the level at which he did, Jack had found his old partners steadily slipping away. His commitment to extreme climbing was total and as his partners developed other interests they and he both realised the tremendous gap between the good and the great in climbing. No-one can stay at the extreme level unless his mind is completely occupied with it, and as his partners began to be more and more concerned with business, families and the usual worldly cares, Jack had found them gradually dropping out of his climbing life. Most of them had remained as friends, but on a social level, and he had been forced to turn to new partners.

Recently he had had a few unhappy experiences with younger climbers of reputation. Often he had found that the reputation was built upon a very small amount of experience; they were brilliant technicians but had no head for the mountains in general. There had been conflicts and the old feeling of relating totally to his partner was gone. Some of these climbers seemed to be with him not for the sake of the prospective route but in order to try and be better than him, to show him lacking in some technical aspect. He knew he was something of an idol to many mountaineers and that there are always those who seek to destroy idols but often he had been surprised by the blatantness of this attitude in some of those whom he had climbed with. It was as if the mountain was purely incidental and the reason for being there was competition on the human level. The mountains themselves had a way of taking care of misconceptions: this type of climber was usually dropped quickly both by Jack and the mountains. But it had made him wary, for he knew he would have to seek a relatively strange partner, and that this was potentially the greatest disaster area in what was already a dangerous business.

John Dunlop had been in his line of vision for most of his short career. Jack had watched his meteoric progress with the close interest that he took in anyone who looked as if he was moving into the upper levels of the sport. From the routes he was doing and his way of doing them, from the several hours they had spent talking over meals, beers and bottles of wine, and from doing some rock climbs together, Jack had come to the conclusion that in John he had found a kindred spirit. True, he was young but while confident in his powers he did not have the arrogance of the limited mind that thinks because he has reached a certain level then everything is easy. John seemed to know that while he was very good and had done a lot, there was still an incredible amount to learn in the mountaineering world.

Watching people under stress for some eighteen years had made Jack pretty aware of people's potential for behaviour in dangerous circumstances even after a few conversations, and he had been impressed by the underlying calm and emotional control that John showed in everyday life.

Jack had considered asking him to come on the Jorasses climb after their last meeting at the end of the summer season, but had given himself a few weeks to let the decision mature and see if there were any negatives he had overlooked in his calculated liking of John.

But no cracks had appeared. On the contrary, his feelings were unexpectedly confirmed late in September.

During his photographic survey of the route Jack had remembered that the ubiquitous Charlie Wilson had a magnificent photo of the spur taken from a helicopter the previous winter when he was checking out possible filming locations in the Mont Blanc range. On request Charlie sent him a copy, appending a note in which he wrote:

" . . . Saw John Dunlop burn up a new route on Aonach Dubh yesterday—some performance: solo, especially as he was cut up that George has stopped climbing. Keep an eye out for him in Cham. this winter . . ."

Two days later Jack sent the telegram. The returning phone call had been brief and to the point: there had been no need to discuss training methods. Each knew the other would arrive in good shape.

Jack was out on one of his favourite occupations, ski touring in search of powder snow. Ski touring is the best way of moving through mountains when there is a lot of snow and walking would be difficult. To the base of your skis you attach a length of skin, usually sealskin, which adheres to the snow when moving uphill. With a moveable heel piece on the

ski bindings you get into a steady rhythm and can move surprisingly easily through all kind of mountainous terrain. When
the uphill is finished and you are ready for the descent you
simply take off the skins, lock the pieces into the downhill
position and off you go.

That evening Jack was aiming for the summit of La Riondaz, whose steep face provided one of the great runs of
Leysin although it was often out of condition due to avalanche danger. It had been extremely cold during the day and
the sun had made hardly any impression on the powder,
which was dry and light on top of a hard base: almost ideal
off-piste conditions. Taking off his skis he scrambled up the
last part to the summit on foot and stood there for a time
looking at the descent. There was a slight danger of avalanche but it did not look as if the whole slope would go, and
Jack reckoned he could outrun any small slides.

Checking his bindings carefully he gave a last glance at the
clouded valley and pushed out on to the slope. The top part
was steep and a few sharp jump turns were needed before he
came on to the wide centre part and could settle into an easy
rhythm.

There is something almost sexual about powder skiing. A
rush of delight went to Jack's head and he found himself
crying out loud from sheer pleasure, all other thoughts and
cares chased from his mind.

The Alps were spread out in front of him and the evening
silence was almost complete with only the swish of his breathing and his skis to disturb it. Conditions were ideal and he
hardly needed any effort to turn the skis: they almost
seemed to be turning him instead of the other way round.

Suddenly and violently, another noise intruded upon his
euphoric state, a noise he knew only too well. His reactions
were fast and automatic as the whole slope to his right began
to move. Down and to the left everything was still stable:
checking in mid-turn he pointed his skis down and, going
very fast, reached the safety of a boulder. He flung in a rapid
turn and, with the calm that characterised all his climbing
movements, leant easily on his poles and watched the slope
he had just descended passing with a rush about twenty
metres away. As it was early in the season, the base had not

adhered to the grass slope beneath and the steep top part had come away.

"Ah well," he muttered to himself, "can't be right all the time. The rest of the run should be safe." He moved off on to the now powderless track of the avalanche. At the bottom he had to slalom through a few large lumps before he was into the trees and deep powder again. In places it was steep and in the gloom he bounced over one or two small cliffs, but he had skied this part so many times he could have done it blindfold. His pleasure returned. Going fast and non-stop he closed in on the lights of the village, crossed a road, jumped a fence, threw in a few tight turns down a steep bank and, checking fast, pulled up in front of a chalet style building with a large sign saying Club Vagabond on the front.

Feeling like a beer after the exhilaration of the descent he released his bindings, pulled open the door and stopped in the reception area to take off his high plastic boots before going to the bar. The attractive, black-haired receptionist glanced up idly, expecting just another customer. But when she saw the tall blond figure her eyes lit up.

"Jack, love! Haven't seen you for ages. Where have you been hiding?"

"Nowhere, Susi," laughed Jack. "Just been doing some work on the chalet. Seems autumn's the only time of the year when I can find enough time. Anyway you know the telephone number if you want to see me."

It was Susie's turn to laugh. "I'm an old-fashioned girl, Jack. I like to be invited. Anyway, I'd never know what I'd be disturbing!"

"What do you mean, disturbing? There's just me and the dog down there: you'd be welcome any time."

A little seriousness crept into Susie's voice. "Yes, I know: that's the trouble. But I don't really know what I'd be letting myself in for. Your reputation in other fields isn't as good as your climbing one, Jack McDonald."

"Come on, Susie, that's bullshit and you know it. A guy can't live alone all the time and you know how rumour flies around this place. If I took a piss in my back garden people in the Vag would hear about it before it hit the ground."

"Yeah, you may be right . . . but most rumour has a basis

of fact, exaggerated or not. Be that as it may, I was going to call you tonight. We're having a party at our chalet tonight and you're high on the invitation list. Part two is that if you're going downstairs, Joan's in the bar."

Jack's face clouded a little. "Thanks for the invite. And the warning. I'll drop by tonight: I feel like some relaxation. But I came for a beer: it doesn't really matter who's in the bar. See you later, love."

Wondering what Joan, his ex-wife, wanted, he went downstairs leaving the receptionist to her thoughts which, if he had known them, might even have stopped his quest for the much-desired beer.

Jack was attractive to women and knew it, like he knew most things about himself. He had married ten years previously, but the marriage had lasted only half that time. At the beginning it had been almost idealistically happy, but slowly the strain of extreme climbing began to tell. It became more and more apparent to Joan that she was number two in Jack's life, mountains claiming first place, and as the years went by she found it increasingly unacceptable. There were long periods of separation when Jack was in the Himalayas, and the inevitable affairs on both sides. But it was not the latter that had killed the relationship: they had long before learned to handle transitory affairs and one night urges. But Jack was totally occupied with climbing plans and Joan, a very beautiful and independent woman, was not used to taking second place to anyone or anything. Slowly the love turned to dislike and hostility.

Jack knew that bad feeling would affect his climbing. Tackling a problem in the upper levels of mountaineering you cannot afford to have other thoughts chasing through your mind. Concentration on the matter in hand needs to be absolute and nothing is more capable of distracting it than an emotional problem continually plaguing your mind.

So Jack had made his decision. It was not an easy one but his mountaineering experience had made him used to taking hard and serious decisions quickly and definitively. One day he said to Joan:

"It's finished. I want a divorce. Don't worry about the financial aspect: I'll provide a settlement."

Despite her pain at such peremptory dismissal Joan agreed, for the situation was rapidly becoming intolerable for her. Jack had independent means as well as earning enough from his work to live very comfortably, and he was generous. She moved into the world again as a free woman with enough to live well.

At first the release had been good and she had had a wild time running around enjoying herself. But as the boy friends came and went she realised, slowly but surely, that none of them matched up to Jack. She met so many weak men that she began to wonder if most of them were like that, and to long to come across a strong independent man again. So far the search had been unsuccessful and she periodically drifted back to Leysin to see Jack, though without revealing her real reasons. Usually there was a boy friend in tow: she hated to travel alone.

Quick-minded as ever, Jack had become aware of what was happening but he did not care to attempt a repeat performance. Knowing that no long term relationship could stand up to his way of life, he had a series of girlfriends who knew exactly how he felt. He went to see them and they came to see him, but essentially he lived alone and always would. As he was an attractive man, finding girlfriends was no problem, and he seemed to have better luck than Joan. Some of his best friends were women, mostly intelligent, independent and without illusions. Often preferring their company to men, he had one thing in common with his ex-wife: he had begun to doubt so-called male superiority. Some of his girlfriends seemed to have a much harder appreciation of what went on in life than men. He had watched so many of his male friends fall to pieces under emotional strain. . .

Most people by the bar greeted him as he walked in, but he did not stop to talk to them. His wife was standing with two men. As he hugged Joan he felt a flicker of inward amusement at the company she had chosen.

"Hi, you're looking as fine as ever. Hello Lucien, hello Hans."

There was no need for introductions. Lucien was a very good friend and Hans a ski instructor from Diablerets whom he knew reasonably well. But the reason for his amusement was the bizarre make up of the trio. Lucien was a homosexual Frenchman, the director of a publishing firm in Paris, whom he had known for about five years. They had a common interest in books and classical music and often had meals and discussions together. They frequently talked about their friends, Jack's women and Lucien's men, but there was nothing between them on the sexual level: homosexuality played no part in Jack's make up and Lucien knew it.

Jack was intelligent enough to realise that Lucien's way of life was his own concern while Lucien, knowing how socially offensive it was to many people, was very discreet. It was only to friends like Jack that he opened out about the problems that were created for him in trying to live a normal life. Jack had his sensitive side as well as his toughness and appreciated discussing such things, knowing that talking could help Lucien if he was in one of his low moods. But Lucien never remained down or serious for too long: volatile and lively, he was an irrepressible humorist. Jack recognised one of his impish moods as Lucien greeted him.

"Well, Jack my dear, been getting rid of some urges on skis again? One of these days you'll realise that mountains are much nicer to look at than to get involved with."

Jack ducked the obvious conversation potential and said briefly: "One of these days, Lucien, you'll realise what you're missing. Anyway a little skiing might do you some good." He glanced pointedly at the bulge in Lucien's sweater.

It was Lucien's turn to sidestep. "Ah well, we're all getting old, aren't we?" He was a few years older than Jack. "Apropos, isn't it time you gave up this nonsense, Jack? I haven't seen you since the last time you came back. That Himalayan expedition . . . one more good friend gone. It made me start calculating. Do you ever look at statistics? There aren't many empty chambers left in that revolver you keep pointing at your head. Why not write about it instead? I'd be happy to give you an advance."

Still refusing to be drawn, and wondering why Lucien was persistently returning to these potentially lengthy discussion points, Jack laughed.

"I should have known, you old shark; you never change, do you? Professing concern for my health and welfare and all the time you're just drumming up business."

Lucien shrugged elegantly and, realising that he was not going to get Jack to talk seriously, dropped the subject. But Joan persisted.

"Lucien's right, you know. You're losing too many friends and according to the statistics there's a good chance we'll lose you. There's no need for you to climb. And Tom Watson was one of your closest friends—and mine, incidentally. How can you go after that?"

Amazed that Joan was persevering with the subject when he had indicated his dislike of it, Jack nevertheless kept control of himself and, refusing to be drawn, gave a shrug of pretended exasperation.

"For Christ's sake, I'm really touched that you're so concerned about my well-being but all I really came here for was a cold beer and I still haven't had it." He turned to the barman: "A large beer, Jim, and give these people what they're drinking."

Lucien was as amused by the irritation behind the remark as by its sarcasm, but he merely issued an invitation: "Are you going to join us for dinner, Jack? I was going to L'Ours and Joan and Hans have agreed to join me."

"Thanks, but you'll have to excuse me, Lucien love: I still have a lecture to prepare for tomorrow night. But I tell you what, give me a ring when you're at the coffee-cognac stage and I'll come and join you. There's one of the local parties on later too. You might have more success there than here!"

He was alluding to what he had noticed when he came in. Like many homosexuals, Lucien was well dressed and good looking and Joan, tired of her pretty but empty-headed ski instructor, had innocently been making a play for him, while he in turn was quietly doing the same to Hans the instructor.

Hans, young, naive and not too bright, was used to success with women of a type similar to himself, but Joan had completely bowled him over. He could not understand why she was paying so much attention to a plumpish middle-aged man, nor why Jack McDonald had divorced her. An analysis of Lucien's thoughts would have baffled and horrified him still further. He consoled himself by thinking of the stir it would create amongst his friends in Diablerets when he arrived in Joan's Porsche and walked into the local bistro with her on his arm.

Jack had seen the whole comedy of errors as soon as he walked in, and there was no way he wanted to get involved in it. Hoping that things would work themselves out before their coffee, he bade them *"A tout à l'heure,"* and walked home through the cold clear night, almost relieved that he would be dining alone with his old Alsatian.

Recently he preferred his own company more and more, for conversations often took turns like the one he had just left, and he found that usually it took too long and was futile and even offensive trying to point out the apalling ignorance behind some of the questions, or to explain the depth of commitment to his way of life.

It was certainly true that many of his friends were dead and that the finger of fate would be pointed at him one day soon, but it obviously troubled others more than it troubled him. He had never had any worries about dying in the mountains, especially when he had lived such a rich and full life; he did not even think he would be missing too much if it happened the next day. Not that he had a death wish: far from it. But he did realise that in his profession death was a constant companion and, as he sat in his comfortable chalet admiring the silhouettes of the Mont Blanc range and the Dents du Midi against the night sky, he did not feel too worried.

The clang of the phone interrupted his peace. It was Lucien.

"We've just finished dinner and lost the ski instructor. Are you coming over?"

"I'll be right there."

Leaving the dog behind, Jack walked the short distance to the restaurant. It was the kind of night he loved in Leysin: very cold, clear and sharp, with the surrounding mountains bathed in pale moonlight and no sound except the crunch of his feet on the snow. He almost regretted having to go and talk to people, but then he remembered the Vagabond receptionist's thinly veiled hints and the sensual side of his nature came into play. Maybe I'll do something about her tonight, he thought as he arrived at the restaurant.

The air was heavy with the smell of food and people, momentarily an unpleasant contrast to the sharpness outside. But there was surprisingly little noise. L'Ours was one of those restaurants whose success depended on the quality of its food and wines rather than garish gimmicks like folk orchestras or dubious string quartets. Jack often took friends there to eat and the busy patron noticed his entrance, waved, and pointed to a far corner. Joan and Lucien were chatting in a relaxed fashion, mellowed by food and wines. Not wishing to put his foot in anything, Jack asked casually: "Where's Hans?"

Joan gave a gesture of dismissal. "Lucien and I were pretty well monopolising the conversation and each other over dinner and my handsome friend began to sulk. Eventually he said he was bored and asked me to go dancing in Diablerets, which I declined. Fortunately he was too overawed by the atmosphere to make a scene, so he left saying he'd call me later as I'd soon miss him! Exit Hans." She grinned.

"Well, nothing changes," remarked Jack frostily. "What's it to be, *café armagnacs?*"

Waiting for the coffee to arrive Lucien said, "I hear there's a Vagabond party tonight. Are you going?"

Jack nodded. "I said I might drop in. I've been out of contact with the youth of the village for a time. Good to have a few beers with them. It's amazing the odd characters you sometimes meet at parties."

"We all know what particular type of character you end up talking to," Joan commented, half-teasing but with an edge to her voice that betrayed how hurt she felt at Jack's coldness. He gave her a sharp look and, knowing that she had overstepped the mark, she sidetracked: "Do you mind if I join you? As my escort's departed."

"Not at all, dear," mumbled Jack maliciously. "I'm sure you'll find a replacement."

Fortunately the waiter arrived with large glasses of armagnac at the opportune moment and, trivia forgotten, they sank their noses appreciatively close to the amber liquid, a speciality of the house. Fifteen minutes later Joan's Porsche was driving slowly uphill to a creaking old chalet on the outer limits of Leysin. The sounds of heavy rock and loud conversation already lapped at the edges of the night air as they pulled up outside.

The small space was crammed with quadrophonic sound, people, wine fumes and marijuana smoke. Quickly adjusting to the atmosphere, Jack helped himself to a beer from the large fridge and took stock of the situation.

It seemed to be a typical group of young travellers settling in for the beginning of winter, when they would take over the jobs that the Swiss people would not touch: working ski-lifts, washing dishes, tending bars—anything that enabled them to ski and party. Jack often mixed with these groups, finding in their freshness and naivity something attractive that made him remember the wild formative years of his climbing career. Amongst them he could relax more than in so-called maturer company. His fame did not overawe them: they knew him simply as a person who had a few beers with them, smoked the odd pipe, skied powder and was good company. Of course, in that type of company there were many nonentities, people who did nothing and gave nothing, but Jack had a talent for spotting and avoiding them, refusing to be parasitised.

Unnoticed in the dark corner, he watched with amusement as a couple of fast-hustling Australians made a beeline for Joan, while Lucien was casually sidling up to a group of blond Dutchmen. He was about to move on when there was a soft touch on his elbow.

"Glad you could make it."

The attractive face and large dark eyes of Susie, the Vagabond receptionist, looked up at him. Kissing her lightly on the cheek, Jack said easily:

"Well, the very person I came to see. What's on your agenda tonight?"

Laughing, Susie said: "I've already had a lot of wine and a little dope, so I'd say the next thing is you, Jack McDonald. But I've got to attend to my social duties. Are you going to hang around?"

Realising the invitation behind the banter, Jack said: "Sure, there are quite a few people I'd like to talk to. Catch me when you're ready?"

With a quick wink Susie went off to keep on turning out snacks for her perennially hungry guests, while for the next few hours Jack found himself discussing steep couloir skiing with addicts from Colorado. Short skis or long skis, ropes or unroped, avalanches and crevasses: he barely noticed the party thinning out as single people staggered home and couples rolled out into the night supporting each other. More bruises and injuries were sustained on the walks back on the icy roads from these parties than on the ski slopes. Swiss white wine is powerful.

Suddenly remembering Susie, Jack disengaged himself from a conversation that was rapidly losing its logic as wine and grass took their toll, and searched her out. He was brief and to the point.

"Well, old fashioned girl, I'm issuing an invitation. Do you want to come back for a nightcap or stay here?"

Blinking slightly stoned eyes, she smiled; and then they were out in the night, heading for his chalet.

November and December passed pleasantly for Jack. Susie was a good skier and took to accompanying him on his training tours. Life was easy and relaxed, but slowly good physical and mental shape were building up. By the end of December the weather seemed to be settling into a pattern he had seen in previous winters: a few heavy snowfalls throughout November and December followed by long sunny days, with the meteorological office in Geneva Airport reporting a huge area of high pressure over Europe. Just after Christmas he decided to call John Dunlop in Edinburgh.

It did not need a long conversation. John was feeling fit and hyper-keen to go. They would meet in Leysin on January 3rd, arranging for John to bring only his personal climbing gear while Jack prepared the food and hardware. That way they could take off as soon as possible.

CHAPTER 7

MEETING

Cointrin Airport, Geneva, looked its usual aseptic self as
John stepped out of the Swissair DC9 into the sharp January
night. The grey-uniformed Customs officers gave no more
than a cursory glance at the lean figure with two large rucsacs
and then he was through into the arrival hall and clasping
Jack's hand.

"Good shape, I see," said Jack.

"I could say the same for you. How are conditions?" And
the latter remark provided the theme for the conversation on
the way up to Leysin. It's a fairly short drive, taking about an
hour and a half, mainly on motorway with a last steep section
on icy snow-packed roads from Aigle up to Leysin. To John
the mere fact of driving on a switchback road with snow
banks reflecting sharply in the headlights and the occasional
glimpse of a peak against the black sky seemed to bring him
closer to the climb.

For the last two weeks it had been progressively occupying
his thoughts more and more. Living with Judy had been as
pleasant as he had thought. They had kept in shape by going
for long walking weekends and, in December, had spent two
weeks ski touring and climbing snow covered buttresses in
the Cairngorms. Judy had noticed his preoccupation, however, and had gradually found more excuses to stay away
during the last couple of weeks so that his mental training
could be complete as well: tactful behaviour by an intelligent
woman who was aware of the need for good mental, as well
as physical preparation for a big climb. John, unaware of her
sensitivity, pored over pictures of the Jorasses until almost
every rock was imprinted in his mind.

Their parting had been friendly but casual: a brief "See
you" and both went off to very different forms of problem-
solving, Judy to the quiet academic life and a battle with the

sterility of logical positivism, disenchantment with which was giving her a considerable struggle. It was the kind of opposition which exercised her mind to the full because, though she doubted whether she could shake her tutors from what she considered a narrow and rigid viewpoint, she knew that in presenting her case for the possible existence of metaphysics she was sharpening and broadening her own thoughts as well as tackling some extremely accomplished minds at a high level.

And yet as the plane took off, she had a brief spasm of dislike for her enforced involvement with these men, with their well-ordered intelligences and smug self-satisfied ways of life: infinitely preferable to her was the figure winging his way towards Geneva, motivated totally by seemingly irrational impulse, choosing to face nature at its wildest. She allowed herself a rare spasm of self-pity in the knowledge that she had in the last couple of months come very close to him, but would always play a secondary role in the aims of his life, if she were to play any role at all.

But the hardness in her thinking returned. "Oh well, it's been very good and if nothing more happens that will always be something to value," she sighed and switched her mind back to the problems of academic life.

Meanwhile, John was deep in conversation about the Jorasses as they eventually pulled up outside Jack's darkened chalet.

CHAPTER 8

PREPARATIONS

The preparations for a major Alpine climb in winter can sometimes resemble the departure of a Himalayan expedition, and in Jack and John's case probably involved more technical climbing equipment than most big range expeditions.

Alpine winter climbing was still relatively young, for it only got into full swing in 1961, with the first winter ascent of the North Face of the Eiger. Since that momentous date more and more of the great and not so great Alpine walls have succumbed. Initially climbers tended to use the Himalayan style of climbing, fixing ropes and making camps on the walls, for it is difficult to find spells of continuous good weather in winter; but as they began to attempt more difficult winter climbs they became more aware of what the whole subject was about, and came to feel that this form of climbing was unethical and was taking a lot of the challenge out of tackling big walls in winter. One of the most demanding forms of the sport was being downgraded by overcautionary methods. In consequence most climbers subsequently rejected the use of fixed ropes and, using newly-developed special equipment, reverted to climbing with everything on their backs. Though ethically purer, it was by no means as simple as it sounds.

"Put your sac on your back and go." A fine maxim, but there is a limit to how much you can put on your back, and Jack and John were wondering about that limit as they sat in the chalet basement next morning arranging the rucsacs.

Jack had been doing a lot of organising and the gear lay in orderly heaps on the floor. There was far too much to get into two rucsacs.

"I know it'll be O.K. when we get going," John said tentatively, "but are we going to have to do the approach march twice?"

"No," Jack reassured him. "I've made a few arrangements

I didn't elaborate on last night. Let me know what you think."
Squatting on a pile of duvets he quietly outlined his approach
plan. "We're lucky in one respect at least. There's been a lot
of snow in Chamonix and the Vallée Blanche has been open
since Christmas."

"Mm. That's good news," commented John. The Vallée
Blanche is one of the most beautiful and scenic ski runs in
Europe. You can take a téléphérique from Chamonix to the
top of the Aiguille du Midi, ski down the Vallée Blanche
beneath Mont Maudit, Mont Blanc de Tacul and the Grand
Capucin, then drop through the great icefall on to the Mer de
Glace. Glide down the glacier with the Chamonix Aiguilles on
your left and the Aiguille du Dru and Grandes Jorasses on
your right, and you eventually end up back in Chamonix. But
you can also ski down the first part of this run and, just after
the descent from the great icefall, turn right up the Leschaux
glacier to reach the foot of the Grandes Jorasses. This way
they could ski in reasonably quickly, and if they had to retreat or return for more equipment it would be comparatively
simple to leave the heavy equipment at the foot of the wall
and ski out. Had the Vallée Blanche not been open they would
have been faced with an uphill walk from Chamonix on skis
and skins—a long way, even in summer.

"I've arranged for a support team to help pack in the gear
to the foot of the wall," Jack continued, "and they'll make
radio contact at least once a day with the weather forecasts.
They're two American climbers from Colorado, Steve Brooks
and Walter Esher. Have you heard of them?"

"Haven't they been doing a lot of the big walls in Yosemite?"

"That's right," Jack affirmed, "but the point is they're
both excellent skiers. They spent the last three winters on ski
patrol in Aspen, but now they want to take French instruc-
tional qualifications in the spring so they jumped at the
chance of skiing round Chamonix for a couple of weeks.
They're staying at the Vag. at the moment. I've offered to
pay their expenses: I've got a photographic contract for Paris
Match, so that's no problem. And a girlfriend of mine is coming along for the trip."

John was slightly taken aback. He could see that the plan-

ning was impeccable but Jack's sheer professionalism almost
struck a note of discord. All his climbing to date had been
done with the minimum of money and publicity: student
grants do not stretch to extravagant spending, and most of
his contacts with the press relative to climbing had been un-
satisfactory, mainly restricted to answering fatuous questions
at the end of a long night of rescuing. But now he was running into a well-organised mini expedition, with media con-
tracts, support team, radios and expense accounts.

"I can almost see what you're thinking," Jack smiled. "Is
all this circus necessary, right? But if you think hard you'll
see it only involves plusses. As far as staying secret goes we
haven't a chance. The moment we leave the top of the Midi
téléphérique someone'll telephone Jean Mureau at the Echo.
He'll talk to a friend in the helicopter rescue service; next day
our tracks will be seen on the Leschaux and after that we'll
be watched until we reach Chamonix again. And I'm going to
take pictures anyway so we may as well sell them to Paris
Match and give Steve and Walter and Susie a good holiday to
boot."

Laughing at this persuasive line of reasoning, John saw
why Jack was so successful as a lecturer and how he managed
to set up multi-thousand dollar Himalayan expeditions.
"O.K., O.K., I'm convinced. So we break everything into five
loads, ski down to the Leschaux hut tomorrow and pack it in
to the foot of the face the day after, weather permitting?"

"Right, partner."

The face was divided into three sections. First there was a
lower icefield at an estimated angle of up to sixty degrees. It
led to a very steep section of blank-looking rock slabs; but
splitting the stone-swept slabs was one weakness, if such a
word can be used to describe a five-hundred metre ice couloir
at an angle between eighty degrees and overhanging. Jack
knew from observation that the slabs were unclimbable unless
he drilled hundreds of expansion bolts, which he would not
do. Instead, they would try to force a way up the ice couloir,
which looked as if it would take all the modern ice technique
they possessed.

After the ice couloir there was no long term slackening in angle, nor did the difficulties relent. At a slightly easier angle some mixed ground ran up to the headwall, which looked even harder, for the last three hundred metres was a bulging rock buttress split by a chimney crack system.

Having enough equipment to cope with the varied difficulties without overloading themselves created a tremendous problem. For ice they took ten drive-in pitons. About eighteen centimetres long, they can be driven straight into the ice with the advantage that when it comes to taking them out you can unscrew them instead of having to cut all the ice away from round them. These were mainly for protection, while for getting up the ice they had a combination of tools. The days when ice axes were wielded like Irish labourers' spades are long gone. Nowadays you use axes or hammers with picks that actually bite into the ice and hold—hold so well, in fact, that you can take both feet off and swing. For variable ice conditions Jack had chosen a Terrordactyl ice axe and hammer with the pick sharply inclined at about forty-five degrees; with these you can sometimes get purchase by merely hooking the pick when the ice is too thin or unstable to take a conventional pick. But there are some ice conditions in which they do not work, so as a backup a French Simond axe and hammer, better for the less steep ice, were included. Their crampons were rigid American Chouinard twelve points. Most of the time they would be climbing on the front two points, so they threw in a file to sharpen them with.

For rock Jack had a selection of pitons from bongs to knife blades, two aid slings each, forty karabiners and various slings.

On this type of route the leader does a rope length's climbing on two fifty metre perlon ropes. When he reaches a stance he ties one of these ropes to two pitons hammered securely into rock or ice. The second man comes up this rope on jumars carrying the heavy rucsacs and taking out the pitons that the leader has left in place, while the leader is using yet another rope to haul up the second rucsac. Two climbers of equal ability like Jack and John alternate leads, the most efficient method in terms of time and energy: the leader can climb faster because he does not have a huge sac on his back, and the second can almost rest when coming up on jumars, for he does not have to hang on to the rock.

That, then, was how they proposed to climb the wall. The next problem was how to eat and sleep there. Jack, with John's approval, had allowed ten full days' food; it could be stretched to fourteen in an emergency. They found it difficult to tell how long they would be. Winter climbing can be very slow, but given good weather six days seemed a reasonable guess. There was also the long descent down the Italian side to think of, and they certainly had to have enough to sit out a storm on minimum rations. Even then they were not going to eat well: their ten days' worth lay in ten small polythene packs on the floor.

In winter at Alpine altitudes the emphasis of a diet is on heat, energy and the means to offset dehydration. Their unvarying menu would be: breakfast, a few strips of fat bacon, some chocolate, powdered orange juice and lemon tea; lunch, a bar of chocolate and hard candies to keep the saliva going; supper, soup, more bacon and lots of lemon tea.

"It's not enough to get fat on," remarked Jack, knowing John's partiality for good food, "but we won't starve and we'll still be able to climb."

"Looks five star to me," answered John. "I spent last summer on porridge. What about the bedroom?"

The wall looked singularly devoid of ledges. In fact they had only been able to pick out two possibilities. One was what looked like a bergshrund or crevasse where the icefield ran into the rock slabs at the start of the ice couloir, and the other was just below the headwall. For maximum comfort and in case they were caught out on a section with no ledges, they had two comfortable single point suspension hammocks with a nylon tent on top. In these they could sleep in relative comfort literally anywhere on the wall. Light high-quality down sleeping bags and super light closed cell foam pads gave warmth and insulation: only by sleeping and eating well could they hope to be fit enough to withstand the physical strain in such appalling conditions.

For cooking there was a light gas stove with ten cartridges of a special propane/butane mix which would burn in very low temperatures. Melting snow and ice for the necessary drinks can be a long job and this type of stove can be held between your knees or thighs in almost any position.

They were just stowing the last of the equipment away when the Alsatian barked gaily at the sound of footsteps and laughter on the stairs.

"Looks like the arrival of the support team," said Jack, answering the knock on the door. Two Coloradans powered in, big, strong and fit. There were no formalities about the introductions. Slinging a brief 'Hi' to Jack they grabbed John's hand and introduced themselves. John let his hand recover and waited for the rest of the party. Susie came over to be introduced by Jack. Eyeing her speculatively John thought his taste was good but kept a straight face as three more girls crowded into the small room, all with the healthy combination of windburn and suntan that many days spent on the ski slopes brings. They took it in turn to greet Jack French-style, with a brief kiss on each cheek.

"Here's some more of the attractive sights of Leysin, John. Barbara, Helen and Faye."

John was aware of appraising eyes but also of a certain reserve as they formally shook hands. "Well, do I pass, or is a Scotsman such a novelty?"

Half-laughing, half-serious, Barbara burst out: "We didn't quite know what to expect. I think—well, we thought we'd see a huge red-bearded monster. We're all quite used to Mr. Smooth here," pointing with a half-smile at Jack, "but we've heard so many stories about the rough, tough British climbers, and, but," struggling for words she stammered, "you, you're quite presentable." At this the reserve shattered and everyone burst into uncontrolled laughter.

Susie was the first to recover and giving the surprised John a hug, she finally managed to get out: "Take no notice, John. Barbara's never been renowned for her tact. If she met Richard Nixon in the street she'd ask him how was Watergate." At this there was further giggling and laughing.

John had wondered about their support team, imagining some hard competitive skiers trying to outshine the climbers . . . on the way in, but even from this brief episode he could see how relaxed Steve and Walter were. As for the girls, well, with his thought defences down he could imagine a good time in Leysin after the climb.

Susie carried on: "These three aren't here as pretty scenery. We knew that you two hardened singles would probably choke down a rough meal here or eat a quick restaurant steak, talking climbing all the time and re-discussing what you've probably gone over a hundred times already. So we've decided to feed you. You're going to need a really good meal and word's got out around town about your plans, so you wouldn't get a moment's peace in a restaurant. So, dinner's at Barb and Helen's apartment at seven. No other people and we're going to cook up a storm." She turned to Jack: "How does that sound, chief?"

In equally mocking fashion Jack half bowed: "How can I refuse such an impassioned speech or such delicate consideration? Seriously, thanks a lot, girls. We've been too busy to give a thought to tonight but I think you've hit the nail on the head. What do you think, partner?"

"I say we have no choice in the matter."

Jack turned triumphantly to Susie. "That was the first major decision of our partnership. If John had declined I'd have aborted the trip."

"O.K., great." Susie grinned. "We'll leave you guys to talk logistics and go and do the shopping."

"See you later," the four chorused as they disappeared, but Barbara whisked back in again.

"I didn't mean to be rude, John. If I ever meet with a bad accident it'll be from choking with a foot in my mouth, but I'll see if I can make amends tonight. With cooking!" Flashing a cheeky glance she was gone with a wave of her hand.

Instinctively liking this blunt little girl, John was half-dreaming when one of the Americans shook him back to reality with a question about packing. By mid-afternoon everything was finished. Steve and Walter went off for a couple of hours' skiing; Jack returned to his study to finalise his correspondence, and John tried to read a magazine. But looking across in the fading January light to the Mont Blanc range he felt his mind slipping away from the everyday world. No matter how pleasant everything and everyone was, it would be good to be starting the climb the next day. But it would be two more days, days filled with hard work, before they could really start. Accustomed to moving fast and decisively to grab routes in summer, he was for the first time finding it hard to achieve the different mental state needed for major Alpine winter climbs. Even getting to the mountain was a major task. Next day they would descend the Vallée Blanche with sixty-pound packs and walk up the Leschaux glacier on skins to the Leschaux hut for the night. This small hut is usually two and a half hours from the foot of the wall in summer, but in deep powder in winter it could take twice that time. They hoped to spend the second night in a snow cave at the foot of the wall and start at first light the next day, making maximum use of the short daylight hours. There would also be time during the second day to fix any difficult bergschrunds, the huge crevasses that often bar the entrance to a wall where rock meets ice, or ice has split from ice. But all their careful planning would be to no avail if the weather failed, as it was almost bound to do during their week-long climb. Fortunately, it looked to be holding fine as they crunched along the packed snow to the girls' flat that evening, with the stars already bright above them.

The girls lived in an apartment in the lower part of Leysin. The village being built on the side of a hill, it took about fifteen minutes of fast walking before they were knocking at the door. The tall blond Helen answered, looking hot and charming in a full apron.

"Hi, just go in and make yourselves at home, we're just at the crucial stage in the kitchen."

The main room was comfortable and surrounded by books and records. Steve and Walter were already sprawled long-legged in easy chairs, listening to a violin and piano blending in fast but beautiful harmony.

Knowing John's liking for classical music Jack cocked a quizzical eye at him. "You must know this piece."

John came back straight away: "Beethoven's Kreutzer Sonata last movement played by Yehudi Menuhin and Wilhelm Kempf."

Jack nodded, adding an appreciative comment: "Must be the definitive recording of this piece of music. I believe they didn't even rehearse—just sat down and played."

"Maybe if we want to grow old gracefully we should take

to playing music," Steve mused. "Menuhin's a mere young-ster of sixty but Kempf is nearer ninety. It seems to be one form of intellectual activity that keeps your mind constantly alert."

"It's a very physical activity, too," John said. "Both Kempf and Arthur Rubinstein played concert hall concertos in their late eighties and even nineties I believe, and Otto Klemperer was led on to the stage after a stroke in his nineties but still conducted a performance of Beethoven's Ninth Symphony."

"And what'll you be at ninety, a rheumaticky, grumpy old Scot, sitting in front of a fire somewhere in the highlands shouting for whisky and boring a host of grandsons with old climbing stories?" The interruption and change of subject had come from the cheeky Barbara who arrived carrying a tray of chilled Carlsberg Lagers.

"Maybe," answered John reflectively, "if I get that far." He relaxed into a smile: "but I'll have a head full of incredi-ble impressions. And what'll you do? Reminisce about boy-friends?"

Barbara tossed her head: "O.K. Mr. Scotsman, I see you're out for battle but supper calls. I'll tangle with you later."

Jack, amused by the growing affinity between the two, wondered how John would handle Barbara. Both she and Helen were very mature twenty-eight year olds, Barbara a graduate of the University of California in Fine Arts, while Helen had spent six years as a United Airlines air hostess. For the last three years they had worked as cocktail waitresses in Squaw Valley, California, so that they could ski as much as possible and make enough money to travel. That year they had come to Leysin, got an apartment as a base and an old VW Bus for transport and were busy skiing as many resorts as they could and having as good a time as possible. Neither played any pretence games with men. If they liked, well they liked a lot, Jack reflected mellowly, having run full tilt into Helen when she first arrived. Capable and self-contained, these girls could handle good companions without becoming too involved; but if they disliked you that was another matter. Many people took their easy going friendliness as a constant invitation to bed. True, if they were interested in you this was part of the game. But as many a puffed-up type had found, if they did not like or respect you, the put down could be hard and the tongue-lashing severe.

What it amounted to was that they had absolutely no time for phonies and could sniff them out faster than a ferret working a rabbit hole. But Barbara was obviously intrigued by John: Jack smiled to himself at the thought as plates of raw meat began to arrive at the table.

"Great stuff girls," he commented. "Getting into Swiss dishes, huh?"

"We thought Fondue Bourguignone would be easy," wailed Susie, "but we didn't reckon on the sauces. We seem to have been ages making fresh mayonnaise and blending garlic and all sorts of things. Still, it seems all right."

The Americans were looking slightly puzzled at the plates of raw meat, little bowls of sauces and two burners of sizzling oil heated by small spirit stoves.

Jack laughed. "Don't worry, it's not a raw meat feast. What you do is help yourself to some of the sauces. Then you take the long fork, stick a cube of meat on it and put it in the oil. When you think it's cooked you take it out and put it on your plate. Then you change forks, dip it in whichever sauce you fancy and eat."

"Sounds simple," laughed Steve.

"It is," continued Jack, "but don't try to eat the meat straight off the cooking fork, otherwise you won't enjoy anything except fried tongue for a while."

Soon there was only the sound of bubbling oil and appreciative noises until Susie said tentatively: "I know you guys don't want to drink a lot but I thought maybe a glass or two of Pinot Noir du Valais might ease everything down."

"Perfect."

Plates of meat came and went and no-one talked very much. John and Jack ate steadily with thoughts of lean days ahead and the others put it away with the healthy appetites of out-door people. Later they slowly left the table to recline in armchairs or on cushions on the floor, the only noises being replete-sounding male voices, muttering "fantastic", "incredible".

The girls needed no formal compliments. The satisfied figures lying around were indication enough of a job well done.

"Take it easy girls, we'll clean up when we can move," muttered Jack from a deep arm chair.

"You stay where you are," said Helen, "you have enough to do in the next few days. This is a do-nothing evening. Coffee'll be served when the food's gone down a little."

John was sitting on a cushion looking at the records when a figure settled down beside him.

"Well, Scotsman, did we feed you well enough?" It was Barbara.

"I'll ignore that question: the answer's self-evident. But let's say your taste in music is as good as your cooking. When did you get interested in classics?"

Their mutual interest in classical music made the hours pass easily until, with the early start ahead, people began to think of going. Noticing Jack standing up, John started to move as well, when there was a restraining hand on his arm.

"I think Jack's going to take Susie home. You don't have to go, you know." Barbara was looking steadily at him. John returned the look.

"O.K. but remember I've got to be in good shape in the morning."

Barbara laughed. "Don't worry, you'll be asleep and happy by midnight!"

During the evening they had found so many things in common that it seemed perfectly natural to spend the night together. And then they were alone with each other and the night to come.

It was still dark as John let himself quietly out of Barbara's apartment at 4.30 a.m. The stars were still bright and clear and the slight wind cold and sharp as he hunched deeper into the collar of his ski jacket, but to his surprise there was about two or three inches of snow on the ground. Sometime in the very early hours it must have snowed slightly.

Reaching Jack's quickly he found the light on and the smell of bacon strong in the kitchen, where Susie was cooking breakfast and Jack contemplatively gazing out of the window. He waved a casual hand.

"What's this then?" asked John quickly.

"Yeah," answered Jack, "there seems to have been some

frontal activity in the night. I've checked with the Met. office at Geneva airport. It's not serious. A little low pushed its way in between two highs and it's not quite finished yet. They say it'll snow a little more today and clear up tomorrow. But I think we should postpone a day just in case it's worse than they say. We can go over to Chamonix early afternoon, have a quiet night and, if it's good, get the téléphérique and go straight to the foot of the wall, missing out the Leschaux hut. Lucien's got a small chalet in Chamonix and we can stay there tonight. He won't be there, but he always leaves the key in a local cafe with the proprietor."

"Good thinking, partner. We don't lose any time, giving the weather a chance to make up its mind and let the spindrift clear off the wall."

The latter was an allusion to the powder snow which sweeps constantly down faces in winter after snow. Even the slightest fall seems to produce streams of the fine powder that climbers call spindrift. A heavy fall can provide veritable rivers which pour down cracks and couloirs and seem to manage to find a place inside your clothing, no matter how good it is. If there is a wind at all—and there usually is on a winter wall—the spindrift can come whipping in from the side, or even blasting up from below. Seldom a complete stopper, it can be a formidable adversary at times.

There was a crash at the door as Steve and Walter arrived looking pale under their tans and smelling powerfully of beer. Gentle smiles crept across their faces as Jack told them of the change of plan.

"We ran into a party and got about an hour's sleep," Walter yawned. "We got to the Vag. and it started snowing so we kind of thought there might be some revision of plan." He called into the kitchen "How's the coffee, Susie? I've got a mouth like a grizzly's armpit."

"Coming right now, mister. Can you manage breakfast?"

No party could impair the Americans' appetites: plates of bacon and scrambled eggs disappeared rapidly and, at a word from Jack, all four were soon asleep as the snowflakes began to whirl around outside.

As they slept the last of the low pressure was forced away, leaving more snow but a hard metallic blue sky and bright sun at lunchtime. Calling the Met. office from his bedside, Jack received the confirmation he wanted: "There is now an anticyclone over the Alpine areas. Good sunny weather is expected during the next three days."

Though three days is the maximum any weather forecaster will commit himself to, Jack, visualising the chart and reading between the lines, reckoned on at least a week's good weather. By two o'clock they were on the road.

CHAPTER 9

APPROACH

"Jesus Christ," gasped Walter. "I've seen it so many times in books and on slides, but it still looks unreal."

They stood at the top of the Col des Montets with Switzerland behind them and France in front, and the whole sweep of mountains shining in the sun: the north faces of the Droites and the Aiguille Verte, the monolithic Dru, the needle spires of the Chamonix Aiguilles and the rounded summit of Mont Blanc, the highest peak in Europe.

They coasted down out of the sun through the village of Argentière and into the cold valley of Chamonix, snow chains clanking on the unploughed French roads. In summer Chamonix is hot and humid, for at one thousand metres it is comparatively low. It is also usually jam-packed full of people. In winter, especially the months of December and January, it is a singularly unattractive place. True, the scenery above is beautiful but it is much better to be up in it. The town only gets the sun for a few moments in the late afternoon and for the rest of the day both it, and the inhabitants, seem to be permanently in a layer of frost.

As they went to pick up the key at "La Brasserie des Guides", the sun was just dipping out of sight into the hills behind the Aiguille de Bionassey, and they continued up towards Lucien's chalet at the back of the town on the slopes of Le Brevent in shadow. It had been an old peasant's chalet and Lucien had kept the original exterior but furnished the interior in comfortable modern style. Susie and the Americans were going to base themselves there for the duration of the climb.

That night the company was subdued: they ate supper in a local bistro, called Maurice to tell him their plans and were in bed by ten o'clock. The morning was cold and clear, with the sunlight glinting far above, as they waited quietly for the

téléphérique to go up the Aiguille du Midi. For once the téléphérique area was quiet: they had it completely to themselves, except for the attendant who eyed them curiously but
silently.

The Midi téléphérique, the highest in Europe, is one of the
most spectacular feats in this particular field of engineering
anywhere in the world. It goes up in two stages from Chamonix at one thousand metres to the top of the Midi at three
thousand eight hundred metres. The first stage, up to Plan de
l'Aiguille, runs fairly conventionally over steep forest with
pylons in between, but the second sweep, going up an un-
broken swinging arc above the pillars and icefield of the north
face of the Aiguille du Midi, provides a very impressive and
exposed downward vista even for experienced mountaineers.

"I hope the French maintain their téléphériques better
than their roads," commented Steve wryly as they slowed up
to enter the top station, the winter wind buffeting the cabin
from side to side against the wooden ramps.

"I don't care to comment on that," replied Jack, "but
their track record's pretty good. The only real accident on
this part was when some nut of a pilot flew too low across
the Vallée Blanche and cut one of the wires; but as far as I
know there's never been a major technical failure. Anyway,
not to worry: it's our own two legs from now on," as the car
drew to a halt.

Grabbing their equipment they piled out of the car and
started to walk to the exit door opening on the south side of
the mountain. A mechanic came out of one of the control
cabins and glanced at them. A light of recognition flashed in
his eyes as he saw Jack.

"Mais nom de Dieu, Jacques. Ça va?"

"Fine, thanks, Paul. And yourself?" Jack answered in his
fluent French. They had come across each other many times
over the years; Paul allowed Jack to sleep in the workmen's
quarters when he missed the last téléphérique.

"Oh, Ça va." Paul shrugged nonchalantly. "Where are you
off to this time?"

Deciding not to beat about the bush with the word already
out, Jack said "Oh, going to look at the Jorasses. Not sure
what line yet."

The mechanic seemed satisfied. "Good luck is all I can say. When I'm in bed with the wife tonight I'll think about you."

He walked with them as far as the exit door. "Take it easy going down the ridge with those sacs: the steps have been filled in and windblown."

Holding their skis on one shoulder, they shook hands in turn with the friendly mechanic and stepped out into a new world.

Before they could start skiing they had to drop down the ridge from the téléphérique station to the Col du Midi. French-style maintenance was a constant source of amazement to Jack. There was a thick hemp rope handrail with some rickety intermediate wooden poles and steps cut in the ridge; but there was nothing to stop a sudden slip—a slip which would go on for a thousand metres down the north face of the Midi. On a good Spring day, hundreds of skiers went down that rope; Jack had seen kids of four, all types of hysterical people, and even outdoor matrons of seventy struggling down. Amazingly, he had never heard of any accidents. Leading the way he had to kick the steps clear with the heels of his ski boots, clutching the icy rope. Swearing and exclamations came from the Americans behind.

"Jesus Christ," muttered Walter, laughing at the casualness of the French. "In the States you'd have an elevator or a closed tunnel here with a Park Ranger at either end to sign you in and out. What a trip!"

But soon they were sitting on the Col du Midi, happily putting on their skis in the morning sun with the dominating bulk of the great mountain looming on their left: their principal objective, the North Face of the Jorasses. In the slight wind the recent snow was whipping off its summits. Everything was white, even the rocks; but most of this fresh powder would be removed that day.

The Vallée Blanche was smooth and crisp, unmarred except for the double tracks of the early ski patrol. Jack took off, swinging in gentle short turns down virgin snow with the Americans and John and Susie following, each choosing an untracked piece of snow but keeping close to the ski patrol tracks to avoid the danger of crevasses. Even with heavy rucsacs it was glorious, easy skiing. The first part, running under the walls of Mont Blanc du Tacul and Mont Maudit, is wide and just steep enough to carve easy turns. At the great seracs they turned left, carving their way down to the start of the Mer de Glace and from the exit of the seracs it was a smooth run for about a kilometre down to the turn off for the Leschaux Glacier. They had only taken forty-five minutes to this point and had virtually made the run non-stop so it was with some relief to the leg muscles that they stopped to put on the skins. The downhill was over; now it was all up hill to the foot of the wall.

They made a happy group, laughing and joking and, because of the number, Walter, Jack or John were feeling none of the build up of tension that usually precedes a big route. The three-hour uphill walk was long and gentle, first on the enclosed lower Leschaux Glacier and past the corner with the Leschaux hut up on the left bank where Steve, Walter and Susie would spend the night. Then their way steepened, winding in and out of crevasses till about one o'clock they were sitting in the snow beneath their first bergschrund and peering speculatively at the wall.

Little rivers of spindrift ran down the thin ribbon of the ice couloir on to the icefield and poured over its edge into the bergschrund.

"We'd better look for a bivouac cave a little further back," observed Jack, "otherwise we'll be in a flood all night."

It seemed to be one of those days when everything runs smoothly; the first hole that John investigated proved suitable and they spread out to organise the equipment.

In the shade of the wall the winter cold began to make itself felt for the first time. Duvet jackets were donned and John got out the stove to start brewing some tea. Mug steaming in the cold air, Jack finalised instructions to the support team.

"We'll make radio contact at six o'clock every night. Maybe towards day three or four you can take another trip up to the Leschaux hut but you'll have to go up to La Flegère if you want to see the Jorasses. Let Susie handle any French speaking or any journalists who are getting curious. Remember, Susie, to go and see Maurice who'll talk to the helicopter guys and they'll give us the once over when it can be arranged."

In December Jack and Susie had paid a visit to Chamonix and an old friend Maurice, a guide and ski instructor, had arranged to take care of this angle as he was friendly with the helicopter pilots and on call for winter rescues. There was constant watch kept on the mountains, even right through the winter.

"O.K., we're with you," said Steve. "I'll call tonight from the Leschaux to test the radios. Otherwise I think we'll head back for the sun."

With a final wave the three were off, freed from the weight of the heavy packs and carving light, beautiful turns in the knee-deep powder. The excitement of moving fast soon got to them and happy cries drifted back up towards the face as they levelled out into a long schuss on the gentle crossing leading to the right bank of the glacier where they would climb up to the Leschaux hut.

As he watched the carefree figures blasting down to the world of sun and the easy life of a ski resort, Jack felt on the dividing line between two completely different worlds. To make themselves happy, and be able to function easily in the normal world again he and John would also spend the next few days trying to get back to Chamonix, but by a vastly different route. But the motivations of the two climbers were not at all the same.

Jack, very experienced and calm, looked at the wall and the ascent as another few days in the type of environment that gave him the most out of life. He was quietly confident in his ability to get up or down safely no matter what the weather threw at them. The burning compulsion of his youth which had pushed him to his present pinnacle in the world of climbing had been replaced by an urge no less strong but much more controlled, with the maturity of knowledge and decision-making that only years spent learning can give.

Thinking back to his first tangles with Alpine winters, he wondered how John was feeling. There is a coldness and loneliness about this type of climbing which can take a lot of getting used to: it is a very special type of enjoyment. He reckoned that John would adapt easily, or he would not have had him as a partner, but he was aware that the adjustment had to be made and might take time.

In summer in the Alps, even if you are on the hardest climbs, you are always aware that there are hundreds of other climbers at work in close proximity. The glaciers and paths are full of walkers and the skies full of helicopters working on rescues or bringing supplies to the huts.

But in winter there is only the swish of falling spindrift, the winter wall cold which drives into you and your own thoughts.

John seemed calm as he methodically laid out the climbing equipment and, looking quizzically over at Jack, he said: "Do you reckon we should fix the bergschrund? It doesn't look too bad but we could get the heavy iron up on to the icefield and save some morning time."

"Sure. Do you want to lead it?"

Eagerly, John said, "Fine," and with the confidence one would expect: "looks about fifteen minutes' work to me."

The top of the bergschrund was just ahead up the snow slope. John strapped on his crampons, picked up ten pitons and karabiners, tied into the rope, handed it to Jack to belay and advanced to the start looking like some strange hooded medieval warrior with the spikes on his feet, sharply angled Terrordactyls in his hands and scarlet helmet on his head.

His movements were brief and economical: a one-handed swing so that the pick bit, a kick in with the two front points of each foot, a pull up until he was level with the ice axe, a higher swing of the hammer and a mechanical repetition of the movements. On the start of the steep section he had to hang a couple of times on the wrist slings of the axe and hammer, releasing the strain on his hands for a minute. Then with a quick hammer swing he was over the edge and on to the icefield above, cramponning upwards until Jack shouted out there was no more rope. Fixing an ice piton, he untied from the rope, attached it to the piton and shouted to Jack to come up, while he hung from a sling looking at the way ahead.

Jack was soon up with him, carrying a heavy pack filled with all the iron and ropes, and together they studied the foreshortened view ahead. Foreshortening is usually misleading: when you stare straight up a vertical wall it tends to look flat and easy, but neither of them had any illusions.

"We seem to be in for hard work on the ice," commented Jack kicking the black brittle substance he was standing on with his crampon points. "This'll be O.K. but the couloir—well."

John nodded, "I'm glad we brought a file. We're going to want very sharp points up there. I hope there's no spindrift."

"I doubt if you can ever count on that."

As Jack spoke there was a puff of what looked like white dust at the top of the couloir, followed by a long stream running down it on to the icefield. Jack quickly turned his back, crouching slightly out from the slope; John unquestioningly followed suit. A few seconds later there was a rushing and stinging and a huge gust of powder blasted all around them, filling their noses and mouths; but seconds later again there was only the late afternoon silence and tingling cheeks and hands to remind them of their passing visitor.

The wall was clear; no wind ruffled their clothing and the neighbouring peaks were free of the tell-tale spume puffs which normally signify wind or powder snow activity.

"Jesus, where did that come from?" spluttered John.

"I don't know. I've never quite been able to pin logic and reason to the movement of powder snow in winter but you can expect one of those any time."

"O.K.," laughed John in good spirits, "I'll keep my eyes open or closed, whatever's applicable. You know, that looks like a hard roof on the upper rock headwall. It didn't really show up in the pictures but it must be five or six metres horizontal.

"Yeah," muttered Jack. "Good job we brought all that iron. It just goes to show that nothing can ever beat naked eye reconnaissance. Hard to think it'll be a few days before we can get to grips with it. Anyway, let's go and eat."

Grabbing the rope he fixed a descending ring to it, clipped that to his harness and slid back down to the cave to be joined a few minutes later by John. Lying comfortably in their sleeping bags they cooked the evening meal of soup, steaks and lots of tea by the light of a candle which flickered around the powdery stalactites of the roof of their crevasse.

At six Jack pulled out the small transistor radio from his sleeping bag where he had been warming the batteries for better reception. Flicking the button he heard Walter's voice.

"Leschaux to Jorasses, Leschaux to Jorasses. How do you read me? Over."

"Jorasses to Leschaux, Hi Walter. Loud and clear. How about you?"

"Leschaux to Jorasses. Loud and clear too. How's everything up there?"

"Just fine. What are your plans?"

"Tomorrow we'll ski down, spend the day at Chamonix and make contact with a forecast from the Brevent."

"Great. Look forward to hearing you tomorrow. Over and out from Jorasses."

"Out from Leschaux and fantastic best wishes from all of us."

In the silence broken only by the purring of the stove, the outside world seemed light years away. Sleep came easily as the last cup of tea slid down and they were left to the sound of their own breathing and the creaking of the crevasse.

CHAPTER 10

COMPETITION

As they were sleeping peacefully interest was already beginning to develop in the climb. Paul the mechanic phoned Jean Mureau in the Echo de Chamonix on his way home from work, for such snippets of information made the odd hundred francs appear in his mailbox. At the top of the téléphérique he could spot most climbers starting major winter ascents out of Chamonix, and the French press vultures loved the subject, especially after the 1971 tragedy when Gousseault had died and Desmaison had been dramatically rescued in a critical condition on the far side of the Walker Spur. Mureau had heard of Jack's plans but had not known when he was to start, nor with whom; Paul did not know who John was either, but told Mureau about the support team. Promising to keep an eye open to see if they came through again, Paul finished his pastis and wandered home happy through the cold streets with the vague feeling that there was going to be some excitement in the next few days, leaving the reporter to scout around Chamonix, telephone a friend in Flegère to see if anyone turned up to make radio calls, and hire a helicopter to take a look in a couple of days.

Others, too, had heard and the information was swiftly circulating round the Bar National above the noise of the jukebox, arousing a good deal of speculation. But one American was more than interested. When the buzz reached him he stood transfixed.

"Shit," he exclaimed. "He can't do that". He pushed his way quickly to the far corner of the bar and grabbed the sleeve of a young English climber. "Jack McDonald is up the Jorasses," he said quietly but urgently. "Just started."

The young man's eyes widened before glazing over with the cold look of one whose mind is racing. After a minute he downed his beer in one draught.

"Let's go," he said.

In the Leschaux hut Walter was the first to emerge from beneath the huge pile of blankets he had been so happy to crawl under the night before. Padding sleepily to the door to relieve himself he found the sun already up and the sky a deep blue, with a wonderful view on to the sunlit cap of the Chamonix Aiguilles.

Steeped in climbing folklore, the old Leschaux hut had been the scene of many personality conflicts between climbing teams of various nationalities trying for the first ascent of the north face of the Jorasses in the 'thirties. Now a modern aluminium hut had replaced the old wooden one but the atmosphere and the imposing view of the mountain were still there. Walter felt he was looking at something more than just another mountain as he gazed at the shadowy mass in front of him: a huge bulk of blacks, whites and greys blending ultimately into blue with the inevitable spindrift whirling upwards on the summit ridge. Narrowing his eyes he could just make out tracks leading up to the bergschrund. Then, confused and excited, he could have sworn he saw something move on the first icefield but it was too much for the naked eye.

Checking his watch—8.30—he rushed back into the hut for the binoculars, shouting to the others to get up and put some water on.

Steadying his elbows on the balcony, he pointed the glasses at the first icefield. Sure enough his eyes had not been deceiving him. There, already half way up the icefield, were two figures, one belaying and one leading out a rope length.

"Christ, they've got their fingers out," he muttered to himself, and yelled to the others, "Come and see this: they're already truckin'."

The other two came blinking out into the bright day and had a look at the action.

"That's good moving," mumbled Steve, "they must have got up early and started before first light. They certainly seem to be in good shape. Let's get some breakfast and head on down. At this rate we'll have to go round to the Italian side so quickly we won't have much time to go skiing ourselves."

They were right in their assumptions. John and Jack had

started early and by six o'clock had crossed the bergschrund with the aid of head torches and started moving quickly up the ice, alternating leads. The ice though hard, vicious and demanding on the legs, was straightforward. Climbing un-laden the first man was able to move fast until the rope ran out. Then he would secure it and pull up the lighter sac while the second man came up more slowly on jumars carrying the heavy pack. At that stage it was very heavy indeed, for they had not broken out any of the hardware for rock climbing or used any of their climbing food. They said little to each other apart from the necessary commands; but they already felt flowing between them the mutual sense of respect and trust which can only come from efficient and good perfor-mances from both parties on a rope.

At 9.30 they stopped at a stance and looked down to-wards the Leschaux glacier. John caught sight of a glint of glass in the direction of the Leschaux hut.

"Looks like the others are up. They're going to have a good day for skiing."

Jack picked up the ice pitons and started on another rope length. "They're welcome to it. Could be a fantastic day in the sun but I'd still rather be here."

John did not answer but grinned and silently echoed these statements as he paid out the rope. Watching his partner pick his way easily up the ice he could look between his legs at the wall above as Jack balanced out on his millimetres of support points.

What they planned to do, progress permitting, was to make a bivouac site at the top of the icefield, fix their three 50 metre ropes in the couloir and spend a comfortable night. In the morning, before first light they could push on up the ropes, retrieving them on the way and thus making maximum use of the available daylight hours.

Susie, Walter and Steve clambered down the snow-covered slabs from the hut to where they had left their skis on the glacier. The sun was just touching the moraine where the Leschaux joined the Mer de Glace.

"Let's go get some warmth," laughed Walter, stepping into

his bindings. Steve was staring idly down towards the sun, all set to go, when to his surprise two figures previously hidden by the glacier's undulations came into view about five hundred metres away.

"Jesus," he exclaimed, pointing, "would you look at that. They're obviously not just out for a walk." The figures carried what looked like heavy weights on their backs. "Let's go talk to them."

He took off on the easy slope with the others close on his heels. Throwing in a quick turn he stopped beside the mystery pair. As they looked at each other quizzically they found to their mutual surprise they all knew each other. Steve was the first to recover.

"Well hi, Gerry, what are you doing here?"

The climbing world is small and Steve and Walter were turning over quickly in their minds why the pair should be heading for the North Face of the Jorasses in winter. One, Gerry Anderson, was American and in his late twenties; the other Pat Craig, was English and very young, around 21, Steve thought. What were they playing at on this monster of a mountain?

Steve and Walter were among the best American climbers. They had done some of the big, serious walls on El Capitan in Yosemite and a number of good Alpine ascents in the Canadian Bugaboos and Rockies. But during the discussion in the hut the previous night both had admitted to Susie that they were more than impressed with the North Face of the Jorasses in winter.

"I'm glad this time we're only skiers," Steve said honestly. "That's a lovely difficult wall if ever I saw one. Up there in the shadow, there's a certain aura about it. You can feel that wherever you went you'd have a hard time. I reckon you have to have experienced a few Alpine epics before you can contemplate a place like that."

Walter echoed him: "I guess I'd need a good few training routes before I could get the old motor wound up to tackle that wall."

Susie, a non-climber but a girl who was used to mountains, had felt it too in a feminine way: "My heart went out to Jack and John when we were sitting in that cave. I wanted to hug them both and say, "What the hell are you doing here? how can you enjoy the place? when all I felt was as if I was in a haunted house; I just wanted to get out."

As they talked to the other climbers on the sunlit glacier both Steve and Walter were frankly wondering themselves what the hell this particular pair thought they were doing there. They knew their climbing backgrounds. Anderson was from Seattle and had extensive big mountain and expeditionary experience. He had learned his snow and ice climbing on Mount Rainier and from there had graduated on to the mountains of Alaska and the Yukon, climbing such major peaks as Mt McKinley and Mt Logan, the highest and second highest in North America, by their easy routes which were no more than high extensive snow walks. Steve looked at Walter and could see he was thinking the same of Anderson: a lot of mountaineering, but his technical skills could only be average. Nowhere in his record was there a major wall. Concerning his partner. Pat whom they had met in Yosemite the year before there was no questioning his technical ability. They had seen him do some of the short but extremely hard valley crack climbs in good style, and knew that he had been burning around the cliffs of England, free climbing routes that had been climbed previously with the aid of pitons. He had also solo climbed many of the harder Scottish ice gullies but he had absolutely no Alpine experience. Arrogant and cocky about his ability, he had been heard to dismiss some of the big names as "mere snow plodders". A bizarre combination, thought Steve and Walter, but up front they showed nothing.

They chatted about the Vallée Blanche for a few minutes before Anderson finally addressed them directly—

"We heard last night that McDonald and Dunlop were headed this way with three others. Would the others be you?"

Steve nodded, saying nothing.

"What are they on?"

"The right flank of the Walker."

Anderson nodded, "I thought it had to be that. We're headed in that direction ourselves; been waiting for two weeks in Chamonix for conditions."

Wondering what they proposed to do in view of the fact that Jack and John had already started, Steve said lightly

"You're going to have to run then; they're more than half way up the ice field."

At this Craig broke in: "We'll catch them up."

Steve and Walter blinked. They knew what they would have done in the circumstances: turned for something else or gone down. They knew how Jack and John would feel about having a rival team on the wall, but they could say nothing.

Walter tried a vague side tack. "Saw some good new lines up on the Pointe Hélène."

But the others did not catch a glimmer of a hint. Ignoring him, Anderson went on: "We've put a lot of time and planning into getting here and we reckon that it's fair to continue. If we catch up as I think we shall we can always climb separately or maybe the other two might want to join in a foursome." He looked quizzically at his fellow Americans.

Knowing that the latter was extremely unlikely, Steve, his patience going, said, "It looks as if you'll just have to be content with the second ascent."

"We'll see about that" Craig said acidly. "I reckon we'll be at the top of the icefield tonight and they can't be much further than that. Then we'll see."

Not liking the way the conversation was turning Steve and Walter said brusquely:

"Have fun anyway. Let's go, Susie girl." They swooped off for the sun and the Mer de Glace, leaving the others to continue on their upward trail.

Stopping at the junction, Walter burst out, "Christ I can't believe it. I can feel trouble in my bones. That pair should be over on the Aiguilles somewhere. They just don't know what they're letting themselves in for. Jack's going to be really bloody happy." He shook his head, "Sometimes I wonder how people can be so ignorant. Still, at least we can talk to Jack on the radio tonight and tell him what's happening."

Puzzled by the whole incident Susie asked him what was going on.

"I'll tell you over lunch. Let's go." He took off on the long gentle downhill of the Mer de Glace. Seconds later the others were tucked behind him, temporarily forgetting everything as their senses were stimulated first by the long series of rock walls and sharply pinnacled Aiguilles running out into the impressive snow and ice face of the Grands Charmoz on their left, and then by the blinding, bewildering Dru looming up, on their right a huge finger of sun and snow-tinged granite.

Unaware of the developments the two on the wall made good progress. Just after midday Jack ran out the last rope length on the icefield and, as he was almost touching the rocks, pushed his ice axe into what looked like a smallish crevasse. To his surprise he found that both his axe and hand went through unresisting snow. Excavating a little more he found space beneath and sticking his head downwards found a tiny cavern where the crevasse opened up slightly. It looked perfect for two people to lie down in with heads at opposite ends: with a bivouac sac tacked over the surface outside it would give a storm and spindrift proof bivouac where they could be together and cook instead of swinging in separate hammocks. Quickly tying off the rope, he shouted down to John:

"Come on up; I've found the Jorasses Hilton."

Soon John was by his side, thankfully dumping the heavy sac and attaching it to an ice piton.

"Let's have a look then." He stuck his head down the hole. "Fantastic. Tailor made for us." He glanced all round, taking in the steep ice and bald slabs. "It must be the only one for miles."

Munching sweets, they started to prepare the equipment for the serious ice climbing in the couloir. Jack was gazing idly down the sunlit Leschaux glacier when he suddenly spotted two figures coming up, already quite close to the base of the ice field.

"Christ, John, we've got company. Wonder what they're going for. It's got to be the Croz Spur if they're coming up this way." He swore suddenly: "Shit, I hope it's not a rival party for our route."

"It'd be a bastard," John agreed, eyes narrowed, "but much as I hate to think about it, it does seem more likely that they're coming here than going to the Croz. The Croz has already had a winter ascent and this face is one of the best known last great problems. Still, whatever happens they won't get in front of us."

Jack nodded. "I'm afraid you might be right, but you

know the problems a second party can involve you in. If they're good and independent that's fine, but if they're slightly out of their element they start asking if they can use your ropes and pitons and before you know it you're moving at half the pace. It's happened to me a few times."

"Yeah," said John, "me too. But looking at it optimistically, anyone trying or thinking of trying this has got to be all right: there still aren't too many idiots into winter climbing. Anyway, we'll see quite soon." As if forgetting them, he peered up where the couloir started to rear up. "Looks as if we have some work ahead of us."

"Right on," muttered Jack, following his glance. "And it's your shift. We'll do as much as we can—maybe get the heavy gear up to the high point. We should be back about four to get comfortable in our hole."

John started sorting more equipment. He decided to use the two Terrordactyls, for they are at their best on very steep ice. For protection he took ten ice pitons, about twenty karabiners, and some rock pitons and slings: the couloir looked narrow enough for them maybe to get the occasional rock pin fixed on the walls.

Jack fixed two anchor pitons in the hard ice above the bivouac, settled himself comfortably in it up to his waist, leaned his elbows on the lip and steadied the camera. "O.K., ready when you are."

"Fine. Let's see what it's all about."

Through the camera lens it looked really spectacular: crampons and axe points in profile against the Walker Spur and brilliant sky, while the foreground dropped straight from beneath the silhouetted crampons. Progress was of necessity slower than it had been on the icefield but Jack thought John was handling it beautifully as he tiptoed his way across the 70° ice to the start of the couloir.

The picks of the axes seemed to be biting well. There was a slight brittleness on the surface of the ice which shattered at a blow so that the pick bit deeply beneath. So far so good, thought John. He was concentrating fully on the job in hand, unaware of his partner or the wildness of the situation. There was only the ice and the movements needed to make progress.

The Terrordactyl pick is so sharply inclined that you have to be careful as you swing it, or you end up with horribly bruised knuckles. But John was well used to these tools and with an economical snap of his wrist he swung one, then the other, and kicked his front points in, making sure that he had at least three points of contact. The angle steepened up to above 80° and he quickly moved up ten metres or so before his aching muscles demanded a rest.

Time for a piton, he thought. On very steep ice this is not so easily done, for you have to hang on the axe with one hand and try to fix the piton with the other: a very strained position. John swung the axe high above him until it was gripping well, fastened a sling from it to his harness and hung precariously on it. But at least he had both hands free to tap in a drive screw. In a few minutes it was done. Clipped into a karabiner attached to his harness, he hung completely on the piton to give his aching arms and calves a rest while he peered upwards.

The ice continued at roughly the same angle but after about twenty metres there seemed to be a slight laying back where there might possibly be a stance. With a shout to Jack he went on with the muscle-wrenching movements until finally he could haul thankfully over on to a tiny snow ledge with the rock close at hand. Fixing the rope to two rock pitons he called to Jack. "Come on up."

Jack started while John looked down at the great sweep of the Leschaux glacier running into the Mer de Glace, with the Verte rearing up above. Suddenly remembering the other two he peered more closely and found his fears confirmed. A figure appeared over the bergschrund.

"Bad news, Jack. Whoever it is is coming in this direction."

Jack grunted "Shit," and continued jumaring upwards. As he hauled on to the stance he muttered, "Good lead."

John grinned and pointed downwards. "Do you see that? They're not only coming in this direction: it looks as if they're trying to catch us up." A second climber had appeared and was continuing up the icefield.

Jack pulled a face. "Anyone with any sense would have done what we did and stopped at the bottom for the night. They might reach our bivouac site tonight but they're going to be late and we've got the only good place. They're going to have a bad night unless they have hammocks. Even so it's a bad decision when they could have had a good night down below and still caught us up in the morning." He turned to the gully ahead. "Oh well, let's see what I can do with this one."

If anything it was steeper but sometimes, when the ice bulged, Jack could bridge out across it and get some wide legged footholds on rocks at the side. When he reached a stance John joined him and they decided to call it a day. They abseiled back down the fixed ropes to put the final touches to their bivouac cave in the last of the light.

The other party crawled up the ice, slowed down by the long day and their obviously heavy packs. Shaking his head Jack muttered: "They're either going to have to bivouac on the icefield or be here very late indeed."

Cupping his hands he shouted: *"Allo! Qui êtes-vous?"*

In the gently rising wind "How's it going?" came drifting faintly back.

"That sounded like an American accent, didn't it?"

John nodded. "I'd have expected a French party: I wonder who the American can be. Still, they must have met the others so we should hear on the radio. The call should come through well before they reach here."

By the time the sun had dropped down beneath the end of the Chamonix valley they were in their sleeping bags in the crevasse, tight but comfortable with the tent sac nailed to the ice above. The dull red of their roof faded to black; then there was only the faint blue light of the stove as the snow melted, too slowly, as always, for thirsting eyes.

Across on Flégère the support team were sitting on their rucsacs some distance from the téléphérique station not noticing the bitter cold of the January night. Muffled in duvets, they had spent the last hour marvelling at the changing and dying of the colours as the day passed. The call time had been chosen so that they could be sure of making contact with the two on the wall, but they had had to do some undercover work as the ski patrol did not take too kindly to people being out on the slope late at night or descending in the dark. But as good skiers they were looking forward to this little piece of excitement and to avoid perturbing anyone they had simply hidden in an off piste hollow and sat brewing tea as the mountain was gradually closed down. There were no alien presences as Walter opened up shortly before six to give the set a chance to warm up.

"Chamonix to Jorasses. Do you read me? Over."

Nothing but crackling in the icy air.

A few seconds later he repeated the call and there was Jack's voice, apparently right beside him.

"Reading you loud and clear, Walter. What do you have for us?"

"Two things. Good one first. The high pressure's still over Europe. The forecast's the same: good. Did you get that?"

"Read and understood. Great."

"The bad news is that you have competition. Repeat, competition."

"We've seen them. They're still climbing beneath us and are bivouacking on the icefield. I can see their lights. Do you know who they are?"

Walter told him about the morning's encounter.

"That's bad news but they'll just have to fend for themselves," Jack said laconically, and briefly described the day's progress. "Think that's all, Walter. Closing down till 6 tomorrow."

"Out from us, Jack, good going."

In the sudden silence the three sitting in their tree-lined hollow found it hard to imagine the very different situation that their friends were settling into; their remoteness seemed heightened by the very closeness of the contact they had achieved. Packing up quickly they snapped on their head torches and skis, traversed gently across to the piste and began a slow controlled descent to Chamonix with a good meal and a warm chalet awaiting.

In their icy boudoir high on the mountain Jack and John finished their strips of bacon and supped on a last cup of tea talking over the news.

"I don't like it," Jack growled. "They've already made a mistake in pushing on up the icefield. They must really want to catch us up." Easing his head out of the hole he looked down and could see two headlights close together on a stance.

In the night calm a voice came floating up.

"Hey Jack. Jack McDonald, can you hear me?"

Realising that he would have to make contact some time, and that he might as well be civil, Jack called back: "Yeah, I hear you. How's it going, Gerry? We heard on the radio you were coming."

"Are there any bivouac sites up there?"

"No. Nothing but blank ice. You'll have to use hammocks."

"We don't have hammocks."

The information defeated Jack's powers of conversation and patience. "Well, good luck," he called down rather scathingly, and ducked back into the hole as the familiar rustle of a spindrift slide hit the ice above him.

A few seconds later it was pouring down the roof of the tent sac and he could imagine the feeling of the other two as it covered them. They must be pretty miserable at the idea of a night hanging from ice pitons, sitting in tiny steps, he thought; but he felt no sympathy, only annoyance, as he described the situation to John.

"They've already shown that they don't have a true grasp of the situation or what they're up against. Worse still, they're both pig headed. The obvious would have to be stuffed down their throats before they'd be aware of it," he said crossly.

"Well, we'll see what happens," John yawned and, pulling his head deep into his sleeping bag, settled down to sleep.

Jack sat for a while reflecting on the situation. Everything seemed fine; the weather was good and supposedly continuing so; they had climbed well; John was performing O.K. and taking Alpine winter climbing as if he had been doing it for years. There was an easiness in their relationship that promised well. Yet when he thought of the party below a vague irrational feeling of unease crept in before the day's work claimed its reward and he too slid down into his bag to sleep.

About three rope lengths below, the other pair were swearing edgily as they prepared their bivouac. Their only recourse was to hack out a step big enough to sit on, tie themselves to ice pitons and, with their feet in rucsacs and heads in tent sacs, huddle up inside their sleeping bags and try to get some sleep. After two hours' hard hacking they had the bare minimum, enough to get inside their bags and out of the spindrift which was coming down at intermittent intervals. Tired after a long day they collapsed into an uneasy sleep without bothering to make a hot drink.

CHAPTER 11

WEATHER CALCULATIONS

By 5 a.m. there was movement in the snow cave. By candle-light Jack and John slowly crawled back to wakefulness as the stove purred its way towards a first cup of lemon tea. Everything in a winter bivouac takes time; even in a good cave you have to start the day at least two hours before you plan to move. They intended to climb and retrieve the fixed ropes by the light of hand torches so as to be ready for progress in the couloir by first light.

The brew was ready fast, for they had melted the snow the night before, and after the first few sips Jack felt equipped to take a look at the world. Pushing back a corner of the tent sac door he peered out at the still black day. The sharp bite of a gentle wind made his face tingle but the stars, bright and clear, were signalling a continuation of the good weather.

Looking down he could see the lights of the other party gleaming and thought that they must be happy to be moving after a miserable night. He was right: they had been warm enough but had kept slipping off their small icy perches as the edges melted under their body heat. In the early hours Anderson had got tired of trying to sleep and had successfully struggled with the stove so at least they had had a hot drink. Despite their lack of sleep their upward urge was not impaired: slowly and methodically they also went about their preparations for the day.

Jack pulled his head back in to the smell of bacon frying.

"Weather's good," he remarked.

"Great stuff."

Breakfast complete, they began the slow process of getting out of their sleeping bags, carefully brushing the snow off the equipment, and packing their sacs. By seven their crampons were on, the cave cleared, and Jack's jumars clipped on to the rope. A few violent shakes got rid of the spindrift that had stuck on the rope in the night, and it had not iced up; jumars can give trouble on icy ropes, for the teeth of the gripping part of the clamp freeze up and slip, but fortunately everything was in good shape, and Jack's progress was fast.

By the time that sharp lances of sunlight were spearing out from behind the Aiguilles they had reached the top of the ropes. The exposure was already considerable: their downward glances dropped beneath their feet to the bergschrund and the Leschaux glacier far below, a curving sweep and snow and ice whose only scale was provided by the figures below preparing to start. Brief waves of gloved hands were the only greetings exchanged as each leader began cramponning upwards.

"Christ," said John as he launched out on the vertical ice, "I wouldn't like to be in their shoes when I start knocking shit down this gully. There's no way to avoid it when you're out in front."

"Don't worry about it," replied Jack. "It's the chance they've elected to take by trying to catch up so they'll have to take the consequences." He swung on the anchor pitons, laughing. "Have fun, my boy, and don't cut too many of those Scottish steps. I'm going to try and get some good pictures and I don't want ice blocks on my lenses. Or head, for that matter."

"Steps? What steps? I haven't cut a progression step in three years. But don't get too involved in the photography. There's a little bulge up there that looks interesting and I'd appreciate the odd hand on the rope."

Confidence between them was blossoming: combined with their experience in many and varied difficult situations it made their behaviour and performances very natural and relaxed despite the fact that they were on one of the most difficult Alpine faces in full winter conditions, and they were thoroughly enjoying themselves. Both pairs were climbing exceptionally well, John and Jack swinging leads, Pat Craig leading the following party brilliantly. Despite his lack of big route experience there was no doubting his climbing ability, and the couloir was as near to Scottish or American gully climbing as you could find in the Alps: ice, ice and more ice, varying between 70 degrees and overhanging.

The pre-dawn wind had settled; there was an occasional puff of powder but hardly any spindrift, the sky's deep unchanging blue marred only by the vapour trail of a commercial jet. The climbing was serious and difficult but they were all going like bombs: around 3 p.m. Jack finally heaved a Terrordactyl out of the confines of the couloir and at last his view ahead was more than a few metres of blue ice. Five hundred metres of headwall rose almost straight up from his gaze, a continuous line of steep cracks with the roof standing out in challenging fashion about a hundred and fifty metres up. It was roughly what he had expected from the photographs; what was more immediately pressing was to find a bivouac site. At the start of the day he had been resigned to the prospect of a hanging bivouac somewhere on the walls of the couloir but since he had climbed so fast the idea of a comfortable ledge had crept into his thoughts, only to be banished by the sight of fifty metres of broken ground separating him from the start of the headwall. The best possibility looked to be where this met the headwall, but there were no decent ledges there: snow-covered slabs ran almost straight into the wall. There were a few small ledges scattering the top of the couloir itself, but reckoning it better from the point of view of spindrift avalanches to be right under the headwall, he decided to make for it as he tied off the rope and called to John to start jumaring up.

By four they were both underneath the headwall, where they found a shallow sloping ledge below a small overhang: not good enough for lying down or stretching out, but good enough for hammocks. Looking down at the sloping ledges beneath John commented: "I don't envy the others: they're going to have a sitting sloping bivvy by the look of it."

Jack shrugged. "That's their problem."

He still felt uneasy about the other party. He was aware that they had been climbing well and independently, but it had been a day such as he had rarely come across. Almost ideal. That alone aroused his climbing suspicions. He could hardly count the times when he had been lulled into complacency by beautiful cloudless days and fantastic sunsets, times when it had seemed that it could never be bad again; but at night the winds would start the clouds rolling and in the morning it would be snowing and raging as if the good day had in turn never existed. He had enjoyed the day's climbing but was quite prepared for the weather to turn bad, for if it did he knew they could still be in good shape. They could sit out a storm in relative comfort, or continue climbing if it were not so bad. And if—it would be a miracle—*if* it stayed fine they would be out in two days barring unforeseen incidents. Whatever happened they had a good chance of completing the climb, thanks to the many days of intensive and meticulous planning.

But what would happen to the other party if the going got really rough? In his estimation they had already made two errors of judgement, firstly in not having foreseen the need for hammocks, and secondly by their bivouac on the icefield.

Jack said nothing as he watched John stringing up a line of pitons for their hammocks.

"Should be O.K.," John remarked, admiring his handiwork. "We can get the two close together for passing food to and fro and we won't be totally suspended. We'll have one side on the rock and the other supported by the hammock over the side." He glanced at the sun, which had an hour to go before it disappeared. "Shall we have a brew on the ledge before we get into the hammocks? It's been such a fantastic day I'd like to watch all of it."

It was almost windless and they sat on their foampads, comfortably wrapped in duvet jackets and anchored to the pitons, feet dangling over a thousand metres of space with the stove humming away between them. Chatting about the day's climbing, they were interrupted by a head thrusting out of the couloir fifty metres below.

It was Pat Craig, looking as if he had been working hard but cocksure and confident as ever. Jack shouted a greeting, to be answered by:

"Shit, we're going like bombs. Should be on top tomorrow. What's the chances of letting us have a turn at the front?"

Jack did not like it at all. Craig seemed totally ignorant of what they were, or could be, up against. Or, hopefully, he was merely euphoric at finishing the couloir.

"We'll see about that," Jack said flatly, "but you've got to find a bivouac site first."

Tying off the rope, Craig looked round and shouted back: "That's easy. We'll sit it out on one of these ledges here."

Suddenly all conversation was cut short by the violent 'clop clop' of the rotor blades of a jet helicopter.

"Here comes the rescue helicopter," shouted Jack to John. "I bet Maurice is up there having a look at where we've got to. Hang on to the stove, in case it comes in close."

The machine had come in from behind Les Periades and the Vallée Blanche up the Leschaux, and was circling to gain height at the bottom of the Walker Spur, staying well out from the face. Entranced by the skill of the mountain helicopter pilots they watched the wide circles coming higher and closer. When they were roughly level with the top of the couloir the pilot levelled off about a hundred metres out from the wall and slowly climbed up to their altitude to hover.

In the enclosed space the noise was tremendous. The men in the Alouette 3 were easily visible, the pilot, as always, looking straight ahead concentrating on keeping his machine in the air.

To keep the machine hovering looked so simple but in fact it was very difficult and dangerous work. Close to the wall the light machine was totally at the mercy of the violent updraughts and downdraughts always to be found in such positions; the pilot had to work dextrously to keep the machine steady while being prepared to move away as fast as possible if caught by a stray wall current.

Beside him they could see his permanent assistant, not another pilot but a guide and mountain rescue expert, who was looking across with interest at the climbers. In the passenger seats two more figures could be seen, one working very fast with a camera. John and Jack felt very much at ease on their ledge now that they were tuned in to the wall, but as a professional Jack was aware how sensational their positions must look from the helicopter. The guide waved and Jack answered with the diagonal arms 'we're O.K.' signal. In a flash the pilot turned away and disappeared into the setting sun towards Chamonix, leaving them once again locked into the silence of the Jorasses.

"The papers will be full of us tomorrow," muttered Jack,

"and now that they've seen the others the excitement will really begin. They'll make it into a race." He stamped his feet against the wall. "I'm cooling off: shall we get into the bivouac?"

Shortly after sunset they were comfortably installed, while the others had cleared one of the ledges to the right of the top of the couloir and were preparing a sitting bivouac.

John occupied himself with cooking as Jack lay at peace with the world in his sleeping bag, the radio beside him, waiting for the 6 p.m. call. At the exact time he switched on, giving the usual call signs, and was surprised when Walter's voice came booming through from what appeared to be very close at hand.

"Roger, Walter receiving you very loud and clear. Where are you?"

"We're in the Leschaux again. I'm afraid there's a bad forecast and we came up with extra food in case you decided to bail out. Do you want to hear what's going on?"

"O.K. Walter, appreciate your thoughtfulness. What's this forecast?"

"There's a great depression in the North Atlantic which is due in our region tomorrow night but before that there's a small cold front that's already reached central France, it should make its presence felt some time during the night. As I read it, you could get a snow fall tonight with a brief clearing tomorrow but then the big mother should be upon you and you could have severe storms for a couple of days. That's as much as they'd tell us but Steve's going to ski down tomorrow and call Geneva to get a broader picture to see if there's anything good behind. Susie and I will wait here to see what's happening with you. What do you think of that? Over."

"Thanks, Walter. I agree with you about the weather and your plans. We're in excellent shape and in a good bivouac and if necessary we can sit out three or even four days of bad weather. Have you seen where we are? Over."

"Yeah, we know your position. Fantastic climbing: pity you couldn't get two more days of good weather—it looks as if you could climb out."

"I think you're right but there's an awful lot of difficult

rock ahead and I'm not making any predictions. Can we have a call at 9 in the morning? If the small front's come in we might have to plan some changes but one thing's positive: no thoughts of retreat at the moment."

"O.K., confirm, will call 9 a.m. One thought occurred to me. If you have to climb out in bad weather we could come up the normal route on the Italian side with extra food and meet you on top. I talked it over with Steve and we'd really like to do it just for the hell of it. What do you think? Over."

Thanks again Walter. That's a great offer and we'd like nothing more, but I suggest you hold fire until we see what the weatherman brings us. If it snows heavily it could be desperate even coming up the other side. Any more for us?"

"The only other thing is that interest's building up in Chamonix. The other pair had been talking pretty widely about what they were planning to do and everyone knows that you've both started so they're building it up into some kind of race in the local press. How are relations anyway? I see they're almost up with you."

"So far so good," replied Jack, adding non-commitally but meaningfully, "But bad weather could change a lot of things. Their equipment isn't good enough for a protracted sit-out. Over."

"O.K., read you on that one. If there's nothing else I'll sign out till tomorrow morning. We've borrowed a little transistor radio so can keep you up to date on the frontal progress. Good night from all of us."

"Good thinking about the radio. It's really comforting to have such an efficient ground link. Good night from us till 9. a.m." Switching off, he called to John, for though they were in separate hammocks and tent sacks there was no communication problem. "Did you hear all of that?"

"Yeah. It's the shits when it was all going so well. But you're right, we could easily sit out a big one here." He stuck his hand out with a cup of tea: "Here, get this into you. We'll just have to eat and sleep on it and wait and see what happens."

"Jesus that tea's fantastic. You're right but I reckon we'll get the pitter patter of tiny snow flakes tonight. These fronts don't usually miss the Alps."

For about three hours they drank, ate, and drank until they felt that they had replaced most of the considerable energy used up during the day. Once the stove was out it was deep, dreamless and peaceful sleep, sleep which would not have been so peaceful if they had heard the conversations going on in the bivouac below.

The others were comfortable enough sitting on a ledge with their backs to a sloping wall, feet over the edge, also cooking hot drinks.

"Well, Gerry, we could be out tomorrow. I don't think this Alpine stuff is all that it's cracked up to be," said Craig.

"You're right. You've been doing a fantastic job; the technical leading would be too hard for me but I'm quite happy to follow and take pictures and rest on my organisational laurels. It certainly looks as if we've almost cracked it. I think McDonald and Dunlop should let us lead tomorrow. It's only fair. We've climbed just as well if not better than them. We've taken two days to do what they did in three. I'm going to put it to him tomorrow. I've already mentioned it to McDonald but he didn't comment."

"Sure, right on," answered Craig. "Let's get going really early and if they don't like it we'll climb past them." He looked out at the star filled night. "The weather's great. We can climb up to the base of the wall on head torches and be ready to start the rock at the first stroke of light. I bet the others are so goddammed comfortable in their hammocks that they won't be able to get up in time."

"Great stuff, kid. I reckon us unknowns can give these big names something to think about. McDonald is always so bloody condescending I'd really like to steal a march on him."

With these complex thoughts in their heads they too lapsed into sleep.

CHAPTER 12

ACCIDENT

At midnight Jack woke up feeling a damp pressure on his face. Pulling his hand out from his sleeping bag he pushed upwards. With a sliding noise the pressure was released. Knowing well what was happening he pulled a corner of the tent sack open and peered out. There was no noise, but a lot was going on. When he switched on his head torch the beam ran into a moving wall of white. The forecast was correct in the first part at least.

Hastily closing the corner he heard movements in John's hammock.

"Are you awake, John?"

"Mm, yes," came the sleepy reply. "Am I right in the assumption that the cold front is upon us?"

"You couldn't be more right. It's pretty heavy. Thank Christ we're under an overhang. The spindrift's going to start any minute. The others are certainly going to find out about living in a badly-placed winter bivouac. In another half hour there'll be a spindrift river running down towards the top of the couloir and they're going to be right in it."

"Tough shit," answered John. "I'm comfortable enough, how about you?"

"Just great. And I'm going to take advantage of it, by grabbing as much sleep as possible. Let's postpone our decision till breakfast."

"Fine by me," replied John, and they were huddled back down in their bags.

In the other bivouac the others had also discovered it was snowing.

"Shit," said Anderson, "where in all holy hell did that come from?" He pushed a pile of snow from his tent sack.

"I don't know," grunted Craig, "but at least we've a good ledge."

As he spoke there was a dull thump on their heads and it seemed as if they were suddenly in the middle of a waterfall. The first spindrift avalanches had started. These slides were not strong enough to push them off the wall, and their tent sacks protected them and their down equipment from most of the snow; but the build-up behind kept forcing them off the ledge till they were hanging from their pitons. Constant streams on their heads kept them from getting any of the precious rest they needed after the strenuous day and they spent an uncomfortable night shifting and wriggling. But up under the overhang John and Jack slept soundly, the slides pouring over far out from the ledge.

And so it continued through the night. Before dawn the storm passed on, leaving them thinking it had never existed. The stars once more came through and away in the east the first strips of bitterly cold daylight were beginning to appear.

Both parties started to cook breakfast, but with very different ideas in their heads.

Insofar as the first part of the forecast had been spot-on, Jack thought that the best thing to do would be to fix three rope lengths above them, redescend to the comfortable bivouac and see if the promised big storm arrived. John was in total agreement. Unhurriedly they prepared their morning meal, waiting for first light and the nine o'clock radio call.

The other pair were feverishly preparing some tea and eating cold bacon so that they could be packed and ready to start climbing by first light. A little behind on their schedule, they were sticking to the same plan of trying to get ahead.

"It looks as if the storm was a flash in the pan," commented Anderson. "The snow might slow us down a little but we should still get out, maybe with one more bivouac on the wall."

Craig nodded, hastily gulping tea and packing at the same time. They were ready to start just as dawn broke. Anderson led out the first rope length on the stiff easy mixed ground to John and Jack's bivouac. Their hurried movements aroused Jack's interest.

"Bet they're trying to get ahead. It's shitty tactics and shows the state of their heads but I'm prepared to gamble the first ascent that they won't get very far before the big one breaks. Whatever happens, they're going to have to bivouac in etriers—and they're going to find it isn't so easy in winter as in summer. That's if they're up to climbing the rock, which is a whole lot different than it was yesterday."

But John was worried: "Basically I agree, but what happens if the storm doesn't come in? We're going to find it really difficult to get in front again. In fact impossible, I'd say."

Jack just smiled. "I'm just as worried as you, really. It's a calculated gamble. But I'd back the hunch with all the experience I've had and say that the forecast is correct. Small fronts often miss the Alps but it's extremely unusual for a big depression to disappear without dumping its contents on you. And I think the others are going to run out of steam, get hit by the weather somewhere around the overhang and be so bloody uncomfortable that they're going to have to bale out down here to find a bivouac. Then we can simply say it's our turn in front again."

John could not help but be amused at the calm way that Jack figured out all the pros and cons. He knew from Jack's previous record that it almost took the mountain falling down before he turned back, while his cool behaviour in the face of competition inspired admiration and trust. His fears dispelled, John ducked back into his hammock to continue cooking, waving a brief 'good morning' to Anderson as he came level with their ledge. He listened very interestedly to Jack's conversation.

"Well Gerry," he opened lightly, "in a bit of a rush this morning. Did you have a bad bivouac or something?"

Anderson, serious and grim, normally had little humour and in this situation had none. "As a matter of fact we did. We were sitting in a spindrift avalanche all night but now we're going to make a big push for the top and I think we can get a long way today. Also I think it's about time you let us share some of the leading."

He seemed to be on the defensive, as if expecting trouble, and looked surprised when Jack said: "Well, go ahead Gerry, be our guest, but maybe you should know that the forecast is very bad. Or don't you have radios?"

"No, we don't have anything like that: I'm a great believer in trusting my own nose. Last night's storm didn't turn out to be much and it doesn't look stormy now, does it?" he said stubbornly, pointing out to the cloudless blue sky above the snowy peaks.

Thinking he had done his minimal duty by telling them about the forecast, Jack decided, rather sourly, to leave them to their own devices. It was a decision he was to regret.

Anderson traversed back to a point about twenty-five metres from their bivouac, where the crack system of the headwall started, looking pleased with himself and saying in parting: "Maybe we'll see you tonight."

Jack nodded silently and got back into his sac to drink tea and wait for the 9 a.m. call. On the dot Walter's voice came through strongly, asking them how their night had been.

"Comfortable," replied Jack briefly. "Anything new on the radio?"

"I'm afraid it's bad. The depression's deepened fast and they say it should be on the Alps by early afternoon. This good weather's literally the lull before the storm. Or between the storms if you like. Have your plans changed any?"

"No," he answered, and outlined what they planned to do and what the other party was doing.

"O.K. Understood," said Walter. Steve's all ready to pull out while it's still clear and Susie and I will wait here. What time do you want a call?"

"Usual time. We'll be working most of the day, getting a couple of rope lengths fixed and making our bivouac as storm proof as possible. Closing down till six."

With the others ahead there was no great rush; they sat down swinging tea in hand, watching Craig as he started up the first rope length of the headwall. Gone was the fluid movement of the day before. The whole character of the climbing had changed. Even though there had not been much wind in the night, powder snow was plastered everywhere. Spindrift avalanches poured from the upper part of the wall, usually missing the climbers but sometimes being blown back on to the wall by the slightest breeze. The snow covering the holds had to be cleared away with gloved hands and the moves made with bare fingers. They could see Craig struggling for height, placing a lot of pitons, continuously stopping to put his fingers inside his clothes or blowing on them.

"Now he's finding out what winter climbing is all about," Jack murmured. "He'd better watch his fingers. He doesn't seem to have silk gloves."

Most climbers carried a pair of light silk or thermalwear finger gloves for winter rock climbing as a precaution against frostbite.

Craig's progress was very slow and they could see he was pushing himself on a type of climbing unfamiliar to him. Despite his natural talents, he was finding it hard. He kept shouting down about the difficulty of getting good piton placements. It was not until eleven-thirty that he reached the end of his rope.

"At that rate of progress they'll be lucky to do three rope lengths before nightfall," John commented dryly.

Jack pointed out to the west: "Do you see what I see?"

John followed his gaze and saw long streams of cirrus cloud breaking into the blue on the horizon.

"Oh-oh, it's coming."

"I reckon so. I'm beginning to doubt if we'll ever get climbing at this rate, and they're going to have to bivouac round here if they've any sense at all. Then we'll see . . ."

"Looks like it," agreed John, "but shall we make this place as storm proof as possible? A lot of this ice could be chipped away and then we'd barely be hanging."

"Sure thing. I'll be glad to get out and move my muscles. The old bones are stiffening up."

They began chopping at the ledge system with ice axes while the others continued on their painstaking, upward way. Slowly the sky darkened in the west as the cirrus clouds began to fall out into a general greyness.

"I reckon we've got another hour," said Jack around one o'clock.

By this time they had done wonders with their ledge: by digging lengthways from each end they had managed to create a long, continuous platform with a built-up shelter of snow at either end. It was still narrowish and they kept the hammocks in place to stop themselves rolling off the edge, but they could put their closed cell pads directly on the ledge and lie with their heads on ropes laid against the snow walls.

"I reckon that's about as good a hotel as we can find,"

said John, satisfied. Suddenly his head jerked up as he heard a scraping noise. "Oh, Jesus, I think he's going to come off."

For the past hour Craig had been struggling and fighting for every inch of height, complaining constantly about the lack of piton cracks and occasionally making desperate-looking free moves. Now he was beneath a roof about twenty metres above Anderson, crampons scrabbling, trying to reach one of the only irregularities on this featureless ground: a largish flake which looked as if it might provide a place to sit with a leg astride and give him some rest from the unrelenting wall. The scrabbling stopped and they heard his voice drifting down. It was not calm and there was an almost desperate edge to it.

"Watch out on the rope, Gerry, I'm resting on a very doubtful nut. My hands are almost completely gone and I'm going to have to make a big lunge for the flake. Once I get there, I should be able to rest and get the circulation back. Shit, this is the hardest climbing I've ever done."

"O.K. I'm ready," Anderson called and they could see him huddling closer to his belay, taking a tighter grip on the rope.

Jack grimaced. "I'm not too sure about what he's going for; that flake doesn't look too steady to me. I hope to fuck he doesn't pull it off or take a fall; Anderson's right underneath and his pins don't look that good."

Silhouetted against the sky they could see the outlines of piton eyes with yellow tie-off slings close in to the rock. "Nearly all of them are tied off."

"Like a big zip-fastener ready to be pulled," said John slowly. "Could be a nasty one if he comes off."

Silently they watched Craig start to make tentative moves upwards. They could hear his harsh breathing with the occasional groan which they knew would be from the pain of submitting fingers that could still feel to the deathly rock cold-burning through to the bone. Slowly they could see these fingers searching upwards, clearing what tiny holds there were and groping for the edge of the flake, with the harsh metallic scraping of the crampons in the background. Slowly, tentatively, he came up from a crouched position and finally his fingers touched the end of the flake. They could hear the gasp of relief.

"It's a good hold but I'll have to keep moving: I can hardly feel it."

"Christ, test it," muttered John.

Three pairs of eyes were fixed on Craig as he put his right hand firmly round the lower edge of the flake. With a great scraping of crampons he lunged out, grabbed the top edge with his left hand and started to pull up and over.

That was when things changed for all of them. With a horrible cracking noise the top part of the flake came away, smashed into pieces above Anderson and cascaded all over him. They could hear his cries and the ghastly crack as there was a direct hit on his helmet, but all was cut by the shout from Craig's throat as he started the motions of the almost inevitable fall. Though it only took seconds, it seemed like a slow-motion movie in the aghast eyes of Jack and John. As the top of the flake came away he swung down violently on to his right hand hold. It was still good but his hand was too far gone with the cold to hold properly and he knew he was going to fall. He made a final, desperate lunge to get on to the rest of the flake and missed. The noise of his scream, the terrible rattle of crampons and pitons, the groans of his partner and the violent zip of the protection pitons were to create a lasting impression on the other two. Somehow, one of the protection pitons held and—equally miraculously—Anderson held the fall, but that was the end of the good luck.

Craig bounced about thirty metres and hung motionless on the rope. Anderson's hand groped upwards to lock off his belay figure-of-eight before he, too, slumped motionless, his helmet in pieces, blood beginning to run down his face.

John and Jack stood and looked at each other and slowly back up at the still figures as a cloud tentacle crept over the top of the Jorasses and the first snow flakes began to fall. The fun, the pleasure, the enjoyment of being on the wall had gone. They had a serious emergency on their hands; but how serious they would not know until they reached the others. Whatever happened, they would have to get them down to the ledge and make them comfortable. If their injuries were light and they could help themselves they could be lowered down to a rescue party at the bottom. But from their positions they looked seriously hurt, in which case a major rescue operation would have to be mounted with helicopters, large rescue teams and possibly cables from the summit.

And the wind was rising. Already it was beginning to pick up spindrift and dash it into their faces. The valley of Chamonix darkened, engulfed by a huge area of black cloud. The summit above them disappeared and fresh flakes joined the spindrift in the wind.

Jack gave a disgusted shrug. "Fuck."

John spat. "And no mistake. You've probably had more rescue experience than I have so you'd better call the shots, but as far as I can see the urgent thing is to get up to Craig's body first."

"That's right. I'll lead up"—Jack squinted into the snow—"but it'll take time. Then we'll have to lower them one by one. With a back rope on each as I lower them you can pull them across to the ledge. But if we're not quick, they'll die of exposure."

"What was that?" John snapped.

They both looked up as a groaning noise came from the wall and could see the bundle that was Craig slowly move. There was a sharp cry of pain as he shouted: "Help. Oh shit. Shit. Help. I've broken my leg. My leg."

Jack had to fight hard to get his words to carry against the wind. "Pat, it's O.K. We're coming up to get you. Can you hear me?"

Only the moaning answered, whirling down with the spindrift. "My leg. My leg's broken. Help me."

"Pat, can you hear me?" Jack yelled.

After a pause his voice came weakly: "Yes, I hear you. Jack, my leg's broken. What's happened to Gerry?"

"We don't know, but we're coming up to lower you off. Get into the best position you can; we'll get to you soon."

Despite his leg he was upright on his harness, but what worried Jack was the fact that he seemed unaware that his hands were bare. His gloves were either inside his parka or had been lost in the fall.

"Get your gloves on, Pat," he cried, but Craig slumped forward groaning, apparently unconscious again.

Anderson, in the stance, still had not moved.

Jack turned with a shrug to John: "That's it, old son, it's a major rescue job. Thank Christ we've got the radio. Stick it in your pack, wrapped in a duvet and we can at least get word out, though there won't be anything anyone can do in this weather."

The wind had wound up to storm force and visibility was about thirty metres as cloud surrounded the mountain. Snow began battering the wall, plastering climbers, rocks, ropes and ledges.

During the day John had whipped across the easy ground to the start of the crack in the head wall, leaving a rope in place, and they used it to make their way across, heads bowed against the blast of the wind. John pounded in a couple of extremely secure anchor pitons at the start of the crack and handed a rope end to Jack.

"All yours, friend. I can't say I'm sorry."

Jack checked the equipment, glancing up into the blizzard. "We've got about two hours of daylight. I'll be lucky to make the stance by then. We can still work through the night by headlamps, but watch the time and make radio communication at six. Tell them what's happened and get them to keep their sets open on the hour every hour. But there's nothing anyone except us can do in this weather."

"O.K. Got ya. Good luck," John huddled deeper into his duvet hood, gloved hands gripping the rope firmly.

Making the first tentative moves from the stance Jack knew he was going to have to work hard; but despite the plastering of snow on the holds and the steadily building storm he did not feel on alien ground. Many times, all over the world, he had had to climb difficult rock in storms—both from a climbing and from a rescuing point of view—but never in a situation potentially so complicated. Spindrift was starting to avalanche out from above, but as soon as any big slides lost their initial momentum they were picked up by the wind and blasted round to join the already heavy snow. There was no shelter from it: it attacked from all sides, even blowing up from below.

Jack's face was encased in a silk balaclava with a woollen one on top. The silk covered his nose and mouth to prevent severe chilling but he could still breathe through the fine fabric. His eyes were the only real problem. The snow was coming so fast and thick that goggles could not cope: he had to peer with slitted lids upwards into the maelstrom but every so often a crust of ice built up on his eye lashes and he had to stop to prise them apart with his silk inner gloves. Nevertheless, he made steady, if slow, progress up towards Anderson. Contrary to what Craig had claimed he found the crack fine for pitons and pounded them in steadily, one after the other, moving on in his aid slings—it was no time to think about the niceties of free climbing.

With his back to the wind, John was lost in thought about what they would have to do, occasionally glancing admiringly at his partner. He was witnessing a fine performance and knew it. Jack was climbing the pitch in these atrocious conditions faster and better than Craig in the ideal weather of the morning. That seemed to have been on another planet.

The wind continued to rise. Checking his watch John saw that it was now four-thirty: almost night, though he had not noticed the change as it had been dark grey for the last hours. But the rope still ran steadily through his hands and it looked as if Jack would at least reach Anderson before it got dark.

Jack could see the unconscious Craig slumped in his harness, swinging gently only a few metres to his left. Calling, he got no reply and knew he would have to go up to Anderson's ledge and back down to him. Craig's body, covered in snow, looked lifeless and the right leg hung twisted at a strange angle. Peering more closely through his slitted eyes he saw that Craig's hands were still bare.

"Christ Almighty," he swore to himself, "I've got to get to him fast or he'll lose his hands." They must already have been frozen and every second they were exposed to the terrible cold meant that the inevitable frostbite would be taking deeper hold.

On the last few metres before the ledge he was able to clip a jumar on to the taut rope going down to Craig and give himself some upper protection as he slowly made the necessary moves and pulled over thankfully on to the ledge. Tying himself into the anchor pitons he made a hand signal to John, barely visible through the violent gloom, receiving a wave in return and immediately set about examining Anderson.

With relief, Jack saw that he was still breathing. His plastic helmet was cracked wide open and the balaclava beneath soaked in blood. There had been bleeding from the nose which had dried up and, pushing back the ear-piece, Jack could see that blood had come from the ears too. Feeling Anderson's wrist he could discern a feeble pulse. All the signs were pointing to a fractured skull. There was no way of telling whether it was serious or light. There had been instances of climbers finishing routes with light fractures, but if it was bad then, of course, his hours could be limited and movement dangerous. Working out the plan of action quickly, he realised that John would have to come up the ledge to help him on the next stage of the planned evacuation to the bivouac site.

Slowly everything merged into grey and black as the noise of the storm increased. Jack tied off the rope then waved two hands at John in the 'come on' sign, hoping he would understand as there was no way a shout would carry against the wind; but all seemed to be well and he could see John getting ready to start jumaring upwards. In about fifteen minutes it would be black but with John on the ledge they should at least be able to get the injured climber down to the bivouac.

The fixed rope went tight as John started, using Gibbs ascendeurs as the jumars were bound to slip on the iced-up rope. Jack waited. Looking at Anderson contemplatively he thought about how easily misfortune can creep up suddenly in the mountains. One minute everything can be going well, the next you can be right up against it—and they were certainly up against it. There was little they could do except keep the victims warm. Gently he felt the rest of Anderson's body: there seemed to be no more injuries, but Anderson groaned and began to move slightly.

"Gerry. Can you hear me? Gerry?"

At first there was no reply, but as Jack repeated the question and looked right into his eyes he saw the black gaze clear slowly and a glimmer of recognition appear. The speech that came from the blood-encrusted lips was slow but lucid.

"Jack, Jack McDonald. What happened? Pat? Oh Christ, my head hurts," and he started to bring up his gloved hand.

Jack stopped him. "Hold it, Gerry, I think you have a head

injury. You got hit by a rock. Pat took a fall: he's still below, knocked out. We've got to get down to him."

Anderson's glance was clearing visibly by the second. His speech was slow and slurred and he was obviously in an extreme state of shock but, for the first time, Jack had a faint glimmering of hope that the head injury might not be so serious as he had thought. A scraping of crampons and a twanging on the rope intruded and the snow-covered figure of John, breathing hard, swung on to the ledge.

"Got here as fast as I could," grinned John. "What's the news?" He caught sight of Anderson's open eyes and they both listened as he continued to speak lucidly:

"I feel terrible but I can move—maybe it isn't so bad." He started as if to pull himself into a sitting position.

Jack restrained him. "Take it easy, Gerry, just stay as you are. We've got to get down to Pat before you can do anything." Anderson relaxed into acceptance: head slumped downwards again, he sat quietly, moaning from time to time as John spoke.

"It's about time I did something. I'll get down to Craig and fix him up, then you can lower us both to the ledge. It's better if you make the radio contact from here. It'll soon be six. Incidentally, partner, that was a fantastic lead: one of the finest pieces of climbing I've ever had the privilege to watch."

"O.K. But for Christ's sake, get a pair of gloves on that one before you do anything else: his hands are bare." He did not elaborate in front of Anderson but he could see that John understood from the way he slowly shook his head.

Checking the anchor positions and the way Craig's rope was holding, John quickly made plans.

"You'd better lower me, Jack, then I can have more control over what I'm doing. When I get to him I'll temporarily splint the leg, get him clipped on to my harness and on to my back. Then you lower us both down to the ledge.

"Sounds O.K. Then you jumar back up the rope and we'll get Gerry down. Once that's done we can start thinking about other things. There's about ten minutes to radio call. You get down quickly and get some gloves on Craig and I'll tie you off while I make the call.

"O.K. Ready for action," said John and stepped off the

– 133 –

ledge while Jack ran his rope through heavily gloved hands on to the figure-of-eight which gave him full control over his movements.

To an outside observer their calm and orderly movements would have seemed amazing. It was pitch dark and the storm was blasting great masses of snow up, down and back again. It was no longer possible to differentiate between snowfall and avalanche, for both were happening and both were being caught up in the swirling wind so that the wall was like a mountaineering whirlpool. Visibility was only a few metres and John's head torch cut a feeble stroke into the white. Craig was only ten metres below but it needed full voice to communicate over that distance amongst the clamour of other sounds. John was down quickly, tiptoeing out against the tension of the rope on his front points and, as Jack locked him off, he added a jumar to Craig's taut rope to stop himself swinging and then examined the situation. Jack, meanwhile, carefully brought out the radio from its down covering and opened up. He was a few minutes late: Walter's voice came on the air immediately, slightly distorted but still clear considering the storm.

"Leschaux calling Jorasses. Come in please."

"Jorasses to Leschaux, got you, come in please."

Walter sounded as cheerful as usual. "You're coming through loud and clear. How are you weathering the storm?"

"Good, Walter. But stand by for a long one: are you ready?"

"Ready and waiting."

When Jack told him, Walter's only answer was to swear violently and ask for instructions. Jack thought briefly. "Let's make another call at 8 p.m. There's no point in you rushing down the valley tonight: no-one can do anything. We'll be busy for the next couple of hours but call up and I'll keep you posted. When we get both of them down to our bivouac ledge we'll think again.

"O.K., out from Leschaux and light years of luck to you both."

"Thanks, Walter, we'll need it. Closing down till eight."

Briefly Jack pictured the scene in the hut: the stove roaring, both Walter and Susie lying warmly wrapped in duvets or preparing their evening meal, and the storm outside seeming almost like pleasant background music. It was a tiny luxury which he allowed himself before concentrating on cold, vicious reality. Leaning out from the ledge he shouted into the white painted darkness.

"How's it going, John?"

The answer seemed to spit back in a gust of snow flakes. "O.K. But it's going to be some time before I'm ready to move. Did you make contact?"

Jack shouted back in the affirmative and that he was standing by. He turned to try to tell Anderson what was going on but the latter had not moved and, though still conscious, was obviously in deep shock.

The first thing John did after securing himself was to take off his sac, attach it to the jumar and look for a spare pair of gloves in the light of his head torch. Craig was still passed out but it looked more like a sleep of exhaustion and pain than a coma. His only visible injury was the broken leg. There was a slight bruise on his head but nothing to indicate serious head injuries. But his hands were white and wooden-looking, obviously frostbitten from the exposure during the last couple of hours. They looked badly damaged but the extent of this could not be estimated until much later: the most John could do was to fix some gloves on to them to prevent any further deterioration.

As he was doing so Craig groaned and opened his eyes slowly. John could see bewilderment, surprise, fear and pain flicker over his face, especially when he put up his hands to wipe some of the driving snow from his cheeks.

"Christ, I can't feel my hands," was his first exclamation. "John, it's you. I'm sorry, what a balls up. What the hell are we going to do?"

His speech was lucid, if slow, and despite the obvious shock there was no panic. The characteristics that had made him into a brilliant climber at a very young age were beginning to show. What a pity he's pushed too far too soon, thought John with the first twinge of sympathy he had felt since starting the rescue operation. He was happy that Craig appeared to be taking it calmly: he could not even begin to think what it would have been like with an hysterical victim.

The situation was hard enough with both of them hanging in their harnesses in the dark with the snow raging around and nearly a thousand metres of Grandes Jorasses beneath their feet.

"O.K. Pat, it's bad luck," said John. "But keep your hands inside your duvet and try to get some warmth back into them and I'll splint your leg. It's probably going to hurt like hell, getting down to the ledge. So take this." He had dug out a 'Fortral'—about as strong a pain killer as you can get before morphine—from the first aid kit.

Craig nodded. "O.K. I can bear it. But how do you figure on getting out of here?"

"You're going to have to clip into the back of my harness and drape yourself over my back. Jack'll lower us down to the ledge."

Craig nodded again. "O.K., but I can't help much: my hands are too numb."

"Just relax as much as you can and I'll do the rest."

First he set about splinting the leg as carefully as possible, using an ice axe and the separation bar of one of the hammocks. There was a danger of frostbite here too, and indeed the leg seemed to be numb for Craig merely groaned a little as John lashed on the splints. John then took one of Craig's jumars, attached it on to his own rope, swung Craig's harness round and clipped it on to the back of his own.

"Jack." His voice disappeared upwards into the crack of the storm but the answer came back quite distinctly.

"I hear you, John. What's the news?"

"I'm just about ready for lowering. Can you slacken Craig's rope on the figure-of-eight so that we're both on me. I don't think I'll have to cut his rope—if I get some slack I can untie him."

"O.K." Two minutes later: "Rope free."

There was a slight jerk and with a moan Craig swung round half on to John and half on to his jumar. John untied the tight frozen knot on Craig's harness.

"All right Pat?"

"As all right as I'll ever be. What do you want me to do?"

"Hold on lightly round my neck, so I can take the weight off your upper jumar—then relax on to my harness."

"O.K. Can do."

"Jack!"

"Yeah?"

"Can you start lowering, very very slowly?"

"O.K."

John tried standing braced out with Craig on his back, pushing himself out into the wind with his crampon points scraping against the rock. The wall was slightly less than vertical and he could balance against his front points so that he was not spinning completely free.

"Let her go, Jack."

"O.K., lowering now."

John had practised this manoeuvre many times in rescue instruction, for it was an emergency evacuation method over a short distance. But what a situation in which to have his first real try out! The main strain was on his legs: if he lost contact with his crampon points he would spin directly on to the rope and crash Craig against the wall. This he wanted to avoid at all costs.

Craig was behaving well, not gripping tightly round his neck as victims tend to do but holding only enough to stop himself falling sideways. And so it continued downwards into the unrelenting storm, metre after snow-blasted metre until the weight was lifted from his legs as his crampons found support for all points on the extreme right, near the edge of their bivouac ledge. The relief was enormous.

"Can you stand on one leg for a minute Pat?"

"O.K."

Unclipping Craig from his harness, John anchored him securely to a couple of the pitons on the ledge, got him to sit down and only after he had shouted up to Jack that all was well did he permit himself a deep sigh and a couple of moments' relaxation before helping Craig into a bivouac sac and sleeping bag. The descent must have been painful but he had not complained; the painkiller seemed to be having its effect as he automatically followed John's instructions. Getting inside the tent sac on the constricted ledge was a major effort, for Craig was almost helpless with his broken leg and his useless hands, but at least he was out of the killer storm. Even in his numbed state he could feel great relief as the

Mt. Blanc 4807m

Aig. du Midi

nche

Mt. Blanc Tunnel

Montenvers

Chamonix

SWITZERLAND

battering of the wind and snow ceased. John took off his crampons and loosened his boots so that circulation could recommence, but rest was not due for him yet.

"I'm going to have to leave you, Pat, and go back up to help Jack get Gerry down. Concentrate hard on getting some life back to your hands."

"O.K. John," Craig murmured weakly. "It's a fantastic relief to be here. I can already feel something starting to move in my hands. I hope Gerry's all right."

John did not elaborate. "He's O.K. Just going to need some help in getting down."

Once again he faced into the winter storm. The wind had died down slightly but the rate of snowfall seemed to have increased: it was falling thick and heavy, the plastered rope vanishing upwards like a ghostly umbilical cord.

Three hours had passed in a flash and in the increased stillness he could hear Jack's voice faintly. He shouted up.

"Jack, do you hear me?"

"Clearly John."

"O.K., I'm ready to start jumaring up again."

"O.K. Rope's ready; come on up."

Occupied with the rope handling, Jack had put Walter on standby when he called at eight and nine, and as John started up he told Walter to come on the air in thirty minutes. Anderson had relapsed back into unconsciousness so he had had a lot of time to think during the last few hours. As the rope went taut and John began to jumar up, slowly he reconsidered his conclusions.

There was no way that they could evacuate downwards. It was too great a task for the two of them and the victims might not survive it. Two main alternatives were open. If and when the storm stopped and, more importantly the wind dropped, it was remotely possible that a helicopter could get close enough to drop rescuers and stretchers on a winch wire if they prepared a platform at the top of the couloir fifty metres below. A helicopter could possibly hover there and be far enough out from the wall; but it would demand a very bold and dangerous piece of flying. Or helicopters might land a party on the summit with winch and cable and send them down from the top to take up the injured people on their backs.

But any flying was contingent on the wind dropping and in winter, even in fine weather, there was nearly always a wind on the summit ridges. Ultimately the face drop seemed the more probable even if technically more dangerous. One other solution had crossed his mind if the helicopters could not fly: a rescue team might come up from the Italian side, complete with winches and cables. But it was almost unthinkable that it could be done in time, for the normal route would be plastered in deep snow.

Walter would, anyway, have to get down to Chamonix as quickly as possible and alert the rescue service, but Jack could see no value in asking him to start straight away: better to have a full picture of the situation when they got Anderson down to the ledge before he started.

It took John a weary, snow-clearing half hour to jumar back up to the ledge. He was pulling on to it as Walter came on the radio again.

"Hold it, Walter. John's here."

"Holding."

"Great stuff John." Jack cracked a grin through his ice-encrusted face.

"How goes it?"

John's icicles cracked too as he described what had happened. Jack relayed it to Walter together with his ideas, telling him to come on the air again at mid-night, when they hoped to have both victims down on the ledge. Walter closed down and they were alone again on the immensity of the mountain, swinging gently on the tiny ledge looking at the unconscious Anderson and discussing the best way to get him down.

"We're going to have to use the same system, but it's my turn for the hard work," Jack offered. "I'm well rested now and getting bloody cold to boot."

John acquiesced. "You're welcome, mate. It's bloody hard on the legs. I'll be glad to hold the rope for a bit." He nodded at the inert figure "Craig at least was conscious and behaving well. Could be harder with a dead weight."

"Yeah. We'll have to rig up a couple of chest harnesses to stop him tipping backwards but at least I don't have to worry about a broken leg. His head will be getting the same protection from the spindrift as mine i.e. nil."

They set about the complicated task of getting Anderson out on Jack's back and securely clipped to him, a very delicate operation within the confines of the ledge. Occasionally he moaned but showed no signs of coming to.

Carrying one hundred and seventy pounds' dead weight is no mean task in ideal conditions. Up on the wall, half-standing half-hanging on the small stormswept ledge, it was almost superhuman; but their heads were in good shape and, working slowly and methodically with the odd rest to warm hands and feet, they had the operation set up within a couple of hours. At last Jack was standing braced on the edge of the ledge ready to be lowered on the karabiner-braking system that John had set up.

"Christ, he's heavy. Just lower me real steady John and I'll try to do it in one continuous movement. There ain't no resting place anyway."

John nodded his wild snow-covered head. "All set?"

"O.K.," and the lowering began. They had fixed up two ropes for extra safety as there was so much strain for one. Despite an almost continuous slow movement it took Jack half an hour to reach the wonderful relaxation of the bivouac ledge. He had to keep stopping en route to keep balance—in this type of lowering there is a great danger of losing balance and swinging in helplessly against the rocks, with risk of further injury to the victim as well as yourself. So the tension on your legs is horrendous. Unclipping Anderson from his back and clipping him to a safe piton on the ledge, Jack shouted up to John that everything was fine so far and slumped for five minutes to regain his strength.

A voice came from inside the tent sac. "Is that you John?"

"No, it's Jack. How are you Pat?"

"Shit. Jack I'm sorry about all this. We're in a hell of a mess, I know. I'm feeling better, but how's Gerry?"

"Unconscious. He got hit by a rock." Jack decided that Craig was taking it calmly enough to merit the whole truth: "He has a fractured skull—I'm sure of that but I don't know how bad as yet. He was conscious for a bit but he's under again. I'm going to have to get John down before we can put him in a tent sac."

"Christ, it's all my fault," moaned Craig. "And what now: helicopters?"

Jack was going to have to play it down the line on the radio, so he outlined his plans.

"Shit," Craig said and relapsed into silence as Jack made contact with John and told him to come down. In a few minutes the ghostly snowclad figure slithered on to the ledge, appearing like a vision out of the storm. The snow was falling thick and fast but the wind had dropped to near zero. The only noise apart from their own was the rushing of avalanches down the central couloir and the slides tipping off the overhang above their heads on to the icefield below.

Jack got out the radio to call Walter and Anderson chose this moment to come to again, groaning but lucid.

"What's happened. Where am I?"

He seemed to be suffering from partial loss of memory but Craig looked over and patiently explained the situation while Jack got out the radio and spoke to Walter.

"I reckon you and Susie should start on down now," he finished. "It'll be a long haul in the dark but you should get down to Chamonix by early morning in time to alert someone at the gendarmerie. We'll open up on the hour every hour. They have a huge radio down there and they should be able to make direct contact with us."

"We'll get going as soon as possible. I'd suggest opening up from 6 a.m. onwards: it'll be slow going in this whiteout. I can only say 'fantastic' from Susie and me."

"Take it easy going down."

"We shall. Don't worry. In the meantime, out until morning."

"Out from the Jorasses."

Once again the tenuous thread to civilisation was snapped and the four figures shut off behind their curtain of snow. Both Jack and John were weary from their hours of work but there was no rest in sight for either. With Anderson conscious it was easier to get him into the other tent sac and they decided to squeeze their patients into separate tent sacs, Anderson with Jack and Craig with John, and start getting some hot drinks going and tending to their wounds.

Their situations were very cramped but a hundred times

better than out on the wall. The first thing to do was to brush out all the powder snow from the tent sacs with their little brushes so it did not melt inside, a laborious task in itself. The victims could not be undressed to get into sleeping bags so once all their clothing had been meticulously cleaned, they slid the sleeping bags on over this keeping their boots on to be in a state of instant readiness for evacuation. Craig was in a lot of pain with his leg, but bore it with only the odd involuntary groan when John touched it. His hands were hurting badly too, but at least this was a sign of life coming back. John inspected them carefully. Blisters were already beginning to form on all the fingers.

"Thank Christ," he thought. Although they were still utterly useless and had to be kept warm, and he would have to have extensive treatment, it meant that if they could be kept in this state amputation could probably be avoided, unless infection set in.

Phase one of the rescue was over—the victims would not die of exposure. But the next, and hardest, part was almost out of their hands. They were eternally thankful for the radios, without which they would have had to beat a retreat to get help, leaving the other two alone, a process that could have taken days with the attendant risk of leaving Anderson and Craig for a long time to think about the seriousness of their situation. While they could be looked after, their spirits could be kept at a reasonable level and their will to survive strong; but when this will to survive goes, as can happen so easily when accident victims are left alone subject to terrible fears and depressions, death is often only a step away.

Both John and Jack were totally involved in the rescue process. They had forgotten about the Jorasses as a climb. It had become a stage in a rescue, with their primary role being to keep the unlucky pair alive until some form of help arrived. The big question was when the storm would give up.

CHAPTER 13

RESCUE

In the Leschaux hut Walter and Susie were getting ready for their journey down to Chamonix. At 2 a.m. Walter was not quite so phlegmatic about the victims' behaviour.

Susie was merely puzzled and slightly bewildered by the turn that the events had taken, but Walter let his feelings come out as they prepared to step out of the warmth of the hut into the night and storm.

"Goddamit, Susie. If only people wouldn't get carried away with their opinions of themselves. How can egos become so inflated that they can ignore reality? Steve and I were better equipped to be on the wall than those two and here we are as a support team. But these assholes trying to push ahead." He pushed the table in a gesture of total disgust—and it seemed to calm him down. "Sorry, old girl, but it is a foul-up and no mistake. Now they're going to trigger off one of the most difficult operations that's ever been mounted, not to count the work that Jack and John have already done—and even if we get the others off they've still got to get down safely. If I know that pair, they'll never accept a winch wire off the face; they'll fight their way down on their own, and I know at least two people who're going to go up as far as they can and try to give them a hand. Oh shit I'm raving. Shall we see if we can get down to Chamonix first? You're going to have to speak a lot of French this morning."

Susie gave him a brief kiss before muffling up in a bala-clava. "That's the least I can do. I don't know, I feel so helpless. I'm so bloody worried about Jack and John despite all I know about them. The others are just mere figures and somehow I can't feel sympathy for them having caused all this. I just hope I won't hold you up on the way down."

Walter liked her subjective appraisal of the situation. He

knew from their talks during the last few days how fond she had become of Jack.

Don't worry, my girl we'll be going like tortoises, what with taking compass bearings and trail breaking, but we'll have to go roped up. There's not many crevasses around but one's enough. Can you handle that?"

Susie nodded. "Yeah. I've been out a few times with Jack and he showed me basic rope handling on glaciers. I can look after you."

"Fine. Getting down to the glacier could be the problem. The snow's so deep that I think we'll avoid the normal traverse and go straight down one of the gullies. Then we'll have a little wade to get our skis and after that we should be all right providing we find the way."

"O.K., I'm ready," muttered Susie. Opening the door they stepped into a heavy muffled night. There was no wind, only a solid wall of white which seemed to bounce back their torch beams.

"Jesus it's going to be worse than I thought," shouted Walter.

And it was bad. Reaching the skis was not too much of a problem but from then on it was a slow crawl. Finding the junction of the Leschaux and Mer de Glace was not difficult— a straight compass bearing till they hit the moraine, and no crevasses to worry about—but going down the Mer de Glace was a creeping nightmare. Feeling their way blind, with only the luminous compass needle to follow and eyes constantly open for crevasse signs, the two bowed figures sloughed into a constantly dissolving wall. The snow was up past their knees even on skis. Occasional large red poles marked the track, and between these and his general memory of the lie of the land Walter could keep a slow course without too many deviations. You have to be very strict in following a compass course in a white-out. Often there is an irrational temptation to go where you think the way is, which often leads to going in circles. But Walter was experienced enough to avoid this. Fortunately he could remember the main features: the long straight run down from the Leschaux Junction, the swing left across to the left bank of the Mer de Glace beneath Montenvers, another swing back right towards the middle and a leftward diagonal sweep down to the exit before the seracs at the bottom. By patient orienteering and working as much as he could with the marker poles he found himself after what seemed like light years at the exit. They had hardly talked: Susie patiently dogged his tracks watching the ropes—but suddenly it was there, the cross over from the glacier to the start of the trail down to Chamonix.

Walter put his arm round her shoulders and stuck his face close. "We've done it, old girl. Jesus, I'd hate to get lost in the Arctic. I feel as if there's nothing but white in the world. We won't lose the way now but we'll have to be bloody careful. Those chutes between the trees could be rattling with avalanches. We'll get rid of the rope but if you hear or see something coming drop diagonally and ski as fast as you can out of any gut. There looked like two real bad spots last time we went down." He peered at his watch. "Christ it's six already. It's going to be light when we get back to Chamonix."

Some kind of luck seemed to be directing them to Chamonix that night: they crossed the avalanche loaded slopes easily, reaching the edges of Chamonix just before daybreak.

At this level, there was a steady half rain, half snow. For a moment they stood shaking themselves then, shouldering their skis, set off feeling like people from another planet, disorientated and strange among the early morning workers going huddled to their daily routine. Engrossed in their cares the latter seemed not to notice the two weary figures, taking them for another pair of crazy skiers.

"Let's go see Jack's friend Maurice," said Walter with a flash of inspiration. "He's a guide and will know exactly who to contact. And I could do with a hot drink before a grilling from gendarmes."

"Good thinking," replied Susie, "I can hardly think in English, far less in French. We should just catch him before he goes off to take his ski class."

Feeling pregnant with news they hurried down towards Maurice's apartment knowing that in the next fifteen minutes merry hell was going to break loose in Chamonix. Stumbling up the stairs of the modern apartment building, they wished they were bearers of better news but reflected that they should be able to get the message over calmly to Maurice, who spoke excellent English.

Maurice answered the door in stockinged feet and ski clothes, the look of puzzlement on his face changing to amazement when he saw how they were and the state they were in.

"Nom de Dieu," he exclaimed. "You look done in. Come in and get that wet gear off and have some coffee." In the manner of one who was used to being called out on many and diverse occasions he added: "It must be bad news of some kind?"

Walter nodded and opened his mouth to start explaining but Maurice cut him short with a gesture. "Get some coffee into you first and then you can tell me."

Stripping off their outer clothes and boots they followed Maurice into the warm kitchen where his attractive wife Hélène quickly shoved two bowls of steaming coffee in their direction. Only after they had demolished these and were being replenished did Maurice indicate that Walter should tell him the news. He sat silently throughout Walter's recital except for the odd gesture and *"Nom de Dieu."*

When Walter had finished he sat still for a moment and said: "Fools. Poor Jack. If only those other idiots had any realisation of what they could trigger off if they get into trouble they would probably never start. Anyway no use moaning about what's already happened. This is a big one and no mistake. I'll call the gendarmerie to get the helicopter brought in from Megève: there's no question of flying yet in this weather but they'd better get here anyway. I'm on the winter rescue squad, so I'd better cancel my class and we'll drive over to the Gendarmerie. At least we can try to make radio contact with the wall and find out what's happening." He gestured to the table. "Just relax and eat what you will while I do the necessary."

Susie and Walter felt warm, comfortable and slightly sleepy in the heat of the kitchen, their night's exertions beginning to make themselves felt. Glad that they had come straight to Maurice, who obviously had everything under control, they were able to think about the four on the wall. It all seemed unreal in the cosy home: difficult to imagine that there were four figures huddled on a microscopic ledge with snow and avalanches all around.

Maurice came back into the room. "Well, the word's out. The helicopter will be here within half an hour. We've got to go over and tell the Chief of Police the full story; he's alerted the other guides. I'll pack a rucsac in case I have to join the helicopter but the forecast is still bad for all of today."

"Can we phone Steve, tell him what's up?" asked Walter.

"Sure, help yourself. It'll take me a few minutes to get ready."

Steve, as disagreably surprised as anyone else, agreed to meet them at the Gendarmerie.

Maurice reappeared carrying a heavily laden rucsac and gave a brief kiss to his wife, who had the resigned look of one who had seen it all before and wished them "Good Luck" as they left. Soon they were sitting drinking more coffee in the Gauloise-filled atmosphere surrounding Chief of Police Gerald Dupré. It was very informal. The gendarmes of Chamonix are mostly mountaineers and actively involved in the rescue service, which provides them with more work than chasing law breakers, and those who were on duty that morning crowded into the small office together with six of Maurice's fellow guides, listening attentively as Dupré repeated Walter's story. The silence was only broken by a few groans as the guides realised the position. When he had finished the chief pointed a Gauloise at Yves Monder, the chief of the guides.

"Well, what do you think? Is a helicopter evacuation possible?"

Monder thought for a minute. "I don't think any of us know the *exact* spot involved, though I'd trust McDonald's opinion. But we need clear weather and a reconnaissance flight before we can make any decisions: it must be difficult flying. Can we have Cressier and Bertrand? They're the most experienced mountain pilots we've got and if they can't do it no one can. And Bertrand flew in the other day."

The Chief allowed himself a smile. "Bertrand's on his way and Cressier's day off has been ruined: he's coming as soon as he can. We'll go up to the control room and start trying radio contact at 10: they can give us more details."

In true French fashion everyone wanted to be in on the act

and the Chief saw no reason to stop them, for they could be asked to don climbing boots and join the rescue party. The control room was impressive. In summer the operations often had to control three helicopters, and that could mean three separate rescues at the same time, so the transmitting-receiving equipment was powerful and elaborate.

The Chief beckoned to Maurice. "Your English is the best. Do you want to transmit?" Picking up the microphone, Maurice put on the head set while the technician pulled the switch to put the transmission into the room on the p.a. so that everyone could hear. They relapsed into silence as the crackling of static came through the speakers. Maurice began to transmit. "Chamonix to Jorasses, Chamonix to Jorasses. Do you read me?"

He repeated it three times: only atmospherics answered him. Looking at the wall clock reading 10 a.m. he remarked, to no one in particular; "Maybe their watches are slow. I'll just stay open for a few minutes and see if they come on the air."

Seconds passed. The clock ticked, the static crackled, and the Gauloise smoke grew thicker in the room, but no one spoke. Each had his own mind on a vision of the scene on the wall and none would have exchanged the warm room for it; yet each of the guides was aware that he might soon be making an attempt to drop into the midst of the savage environment. But breath almost stopped—there it was, faint at first and slightly distorted but still audible; Jack's voice.

"Grandes Jorasses to Chamonix—Grandes Jorasses to Chamonix. If anyone is listening come in please: this is an emergency."

Maurice was speaking immediately. "Chamonix reading you Jack. This is Maurice Aumont from the Gendarmerie, do you read me?"

"Maurice, I read you well. Do you have Walter and Susie with you?"

"Yes, they're here, and we know what's happened and are standing by. What's your news?"

"We had a very uncomfortable night, but we're warm enough. The condition of both men is static, not deteriorating. They're both conscious and fit to be evacuated by air.

But weather's atrocious: wind has started up again slightly and it's snowing heavily. Did you read that?"

"Roger, Jack. We have helicopters standing by to fly the moment the weather breaks. Walter says you think there's a possibility of a winch wire evacuation. Can you confirm that?"

"Yes, if we lower the two men to the top of the couloir it should be possible to get someone in. But obviously that's for the pilot to decide. I assume you'll make a recce flight? Over."

"We'll be checking as soon as we can as to dropping possibilities but we'll also have a team standing by for a summit drop if it's impossible to get someone on to the wall. Over."

"Confirms what I thought. Any other suggestions? Over."

"We'll stay open for five minutes on each hour, but only call us if something is happening and we'll do the same. And let's synchronise watches. I have 10.07."

"Understood, agreed and synchronised. We need to preserve our batteries; out from the wall unless you have anything more."

"No. That's all, Jack. Closing down. Out from Chamonix."

Maurice switched off and turned to face the silent room with a shrug of his shoulder. Monder briskly began giving orders:

"Maurice, you stand by to go on the first flight." He turned to the Chief: "I presume Bertrand is picking up René Souchard en route?"

Dupré nodded. Helicopter teams usually worked in regular pairs and whenever he could Bertrand flew with Souchard to operate the winch which raised and lowered guide and victim. Souchard had been a mechanic before becoming a guide and combined his skills in the very delicate and demanding tasks of helicopter rescue work.

Monder pointed to another guide, Pierre Martin: "Pierre, you stand by to fly in the second helicopter when it arrives. The rest of you get things organised for a potential summit drop with the winches and so on."

Strangely enough, there was never any shortage of volunteers for the dangerous job of landing on walls; and as the pilots got bolder so did the guides on the end of the winch wires. Helicopter rescue advanced in huge leaps, with better machines and more experienced pilots and rescuers as they began to know their working environment more comprehensively.

A clattering of blades and the whirr of a jet engine burst upon everyone's ears. The Chief rushed to the window as the French built Alouette III dropped easily on to the helipad outside. The motor died down slowly and when it stopped the door opened and two figures burst out at a run for the main building. Throwing open the door, the pair stood before the Chief of Police and guides. The winchman looked tanned, fit and healthy like most guides, but the grinning pilot bore little resemblance to what you would expect at the helm of a Gendarmerie helicopter.

Bertrand was in his thirties with a shock of unruly black and grey flecked curly hair. He had flown military helicopters on rescue missions all over the world until three years previously, when he had been seconded to the Gendarmerie for mountain rescue purposes. Since then he had become one of the best mountain rescue pilots in France, sometimes pulling off three or four difficult rescues a day in the busy summer period. Very independent, he did not take easily to discipline and had really developed amidst the relaxed friendship of the mountain people. Clad in jeans and a duvet jacket, with a ski hat perched on his head, he gave the Chief an ironic half-wave, half-salute.

"*Salut, tout le monde.* We seem to have a problem?"

The Police Chief laughed. Bertrand was one of his favourites, despite his unmilitary appearance.

"Yes, you could say that, Bertrand," and the problem was explained once again in the midst of the activity and preparation designed, hopefully, to solve it, while the rain came rattling down on the windows.

On the mountain it was snowing thick and fast. Jack shouted through the intervening layers of canvas: "Did you catch all that, John?"

The answer floated back from well inside a sleeping bag. "I caught it. Looks as if it could be a day of leisure for us."

With that there was silence again except for the hissing of the snow and wind.

Both of the victims were heavily sedated with pain killers which combined with shock, exhaustion and their injuries, made them almost comatose except for some semi-delirious mumblings. Inside the tent sacs things were very cramped, but both Jack and John were warm. After taking off their snow covered outer garments they had shaken them and put them underneath; their outer boots they took off, carefully brushed all the snow from them and put them inside the sleeping bags to stop them freezing. Inner boots were loosened but kept on the feet. Once the victims had been put into their sleeping bags they had taken it in turns to brush every piece of powder snow out of the sacks. Inevitably with the crowding there had to be some condensation build up but by constant brushing and sweeping it was kept down to a bearable level.

John had been euphemistic when he spoke of leisure. With the constant cleaning, cooking and general nursing, neither seemed to have very much time to sit and dream. Spindrift always seems to find its way in, no matter how well you think you have blocked up entrances and exits, while making tea causes the rime which has gathered on the nylon to melt and drip. No matter how careful you are there always seems to be something adverse happening, but as long as you keep working against it a tolerable survival level is attained. But the moment you relax or stop doing these seemingly endless trivial tasks, it is frightening how quickly it can turn from bearable to something verging on mere survival. You fall asleep for an hour—spindrift finds a hole, comes piling in, lies on your sleeping bag, melts with your body warmth and in a flash you have a wet bag which can never be dried out again. On the contrary, it freezes and frozen duvets have about the same warmth as a covering of ice. For the four on the wall, playing the survival game was a full-time occupation.

Craig's hands had come back to agonising life but they were blistered and useless and the main thing was to keep them warm and inactive, which John had done, encasing them in dry gloves inside the sleeping bag. The tissue had been damaged, but as long as there was no more freezing or handling John hoped he would recover everything.

While he was pondering the subject of Craig's hands John

had a thought which had not occurred to him before: he had been too busy with practicalities to indulge in theorising. "What would have happened to the injured two if they'd been alone?"

He could only come up with one answer: death from exposure. Yet now if the weather cleared there was a good chance that they would get out and make a full recovery.

John had been lulled into slight over confidence by the calm way things had been discussed on the radio: of the four on the wall only Jack knew how potentially difficult getting a wire in would be. He had done practice rescue work as part of his guide's training and knew that even in ideal conditions it would be hard to hold the helicopter close to the wall, but he had a lot of respect and admiration for the skill of the mountain rescue pilots. Most of them were of the type he could have imagined flying mail planes in the early days of aviation. Most flying is automated these days but mountain helicopter work still calls for the maximum of human skills in both ability and judgement. Because it is a new field there is constantly room for more experiment as fliers become aware of what they can and cannot do. But they are in a very unpredictable environment; the maximum of skills and judgement can be used by the man behind the machine but a strong wind can cancel everything out in a flash. Jack did not want to allow himself to get optimistic until he actually saw the helicopter in position.

But when that would happen he had no idea, for snow, wind and avalanches continued to rumble and blast around them.

In Chamonix there was an air of general lethargy in the Gendarmerie as the rain kept beating on the windows.

Marc Cressier, the second helicopter pilot, had arrived and been put in the picture. Everything was set to go, and there was nothing to do but wait.

In his office the Chief of Police was discussing another problem with Monder, the chief guide: when to release news of the accident to the press. Dupré knew they knew that there were people on the wall and it was a question of whether to call a conference immediately or wait until they began flying. It was only a matter of time: once the word was out neither he nor Monder would have any peace until it was all over. But the politician in the Police Chief overcame his reluctance to have his peace disturbed, for he knew that the newspapers would get annoyed if they found out he had been withholding a good story. Monder reluctantly agreed. There were only two local newspapers but their reporters would inform the major dailies, and after that the major press agencies would get into it. With an American/Swiss, one American, one Englishman and one Scotsman involved it would be an international story.

He picked up the phone and started dialling.

Just before 1 o'clock the weather forecast was slightly more encouraging: the low pressure area seemed to be moving out, indicating a possibility of the snow stopping in the night.

And so the day passed. The two journalists were briefed; the Chief spent all afternoon on the telephone; guides sat, walked around, read, killed time, and the people on the wall kept surviving. One brief radio call was made to tell Jack about the new weather forecast, giving them a chance to think about the next part of the evacuation: making a platform at the top of the couloir and getting the two injured down into position. But when darkness came it was still snowing on the wall and raining in Chamonix.

In the Edinburgh night Judy Scott was wandering home pondering the latest discussion with her professors. Glancing idly at the bill board of the Evening News her blood ran suddenly cold at the headlines.

"Scot in Alpine Drama. Injured climbers trapped by storm."

Fumbling in her purse for coins she began reading, scarcely aware of the change being pressed into her hand. She hurried to call Charlie in Glencoe.

In a London pub Jack's ex wife was having a drink with a couple of friends when a photo of the North Face of the Jorasses, which she recognised as one very similar to a photo that had hung on their living room wall, flashed on to the screen and the calm precise tones of the B.B.C. announcer explained the situation.

Her first thoughts were as they always would have been: "God, I've got to get to Chamonix."

That evening was a low point in world happenings. The pound had not dropped during the day, no high ranking American politician had been tape recorded in bed with his secretary, and there was temporary internal unity in the French Cabinet. It was a slow news week. There were no world cup ski races in the Alpine countries and by next day many people, climbers and non-climbers alike were scanning their breakfast dailies and or sleepily waiting for the morning news on the radio.

The Chief of Police had finally gone to bed with instructions to his assistant to call him if there was nay improvement in the weather. The guides had gone home but were on telephone alert as all lived in Chamonix, while the two pilots and winchmen were solidly ensconced in sleeping bags in unusual accommodation: temporarily unoccupied cells. . .

Bertrand and his winchman were the only ones with first hand experience of rescue on the North Face of the Grandes Jorasses. In 1973 they had picked up two Germans, one badly injured and one dead from stonefall, on the lower third of the Walker Spur and the previous year they had evacuated an injured Japanese from the same route above the Red Chimney, quite close to the summit. Both rescues had been difficult even under ideal summer conditions and Bertrand was busy explaining to Cressier what he thought the problems would be in the concave bowl of the West Face.

Out on the Walker Spur a pilot is not so prone to up and down draughts but on the face he reckoned they would have problems equivalent to those in that rescuers' nightmare, the concave bowl of the Eiger North Wall. There had been a few rescues made by helicopter on the Eiger, and all were described as technically very difficult and dangerous; but at least on the Eiger they had the advantage of complete documentation of the problem parts of the wall. Climbers had written a great deal about where stonefall occurred, and at that time the rescue pilots had flown many times into the surroundings, so at least they knew something of the air currents.

But on the Jorasses the only previous knowledge they had to go on was Bertrand's photographic flight two days before, when he had stayed well out from the wall. They felt the need for isolation so they could absorb the problem, concentrate on it to the exclusion of the multifarious happenings outside, talk over the technicalities in their own time. What better place to do it than in the basement cells of the Gendarmerie?

Jack and John had established a routine of dozing, cooking, cleaning and talking to their patients. It looked as if Anderson's skull fracture was mild: he was lucid and able to talk about the situation with Jack, only occasionally lapsing into fainting spells. Getting him down to the top of the couloir should not be too great a problem. There had been one amazing example, in 1958, of a Scottish climber who had had his skull fractured on the lower part of the South West Pillar of the Dru but had succeeded in following his partners out in a storm and getting back to Chamonix on his own two feet, but such an effort would not be required of Anderson.

Craig was a different matter. With his leg and frostbitten hands he was almost totally helpless. No matter how carefully they worked, any movement was going to cause him a lot of pain, and if the helicopter could not get a man down it would be doubly bad, for he would have to be carried back up to the bivouac site. It would also, of course, be doubly strenuous for Jack or John, whoever would have to carry him. But he was bearing up well, worried only by the fact that he could not do anything for himself. When he wanted to urinate John had to take everything out for him so he could relieve himself in one of the spare dixies; he had to spoon feed him and hold the tea can to his mouth.

While tending his needs John occasionally thought of Craig's arrogance of merely a day ago, but quickly closed his mind and concentrated on keeping him in as good a shape as possible. Neither Jack nor John gave much thought to what would happen after the rescue: they were totally occupied with the care of their patients and their eventual evacuation. Other thoughts were there occasionally but only in fleeting figments—as on the fine days when they could hardly conceive of a bad one. Locked into their present tense situation they could hardly imagine seeing the light on the other side, though even if the helicopter managed to lift the victims off none of the alternatives to be faced if they decided to get out by themselves—and nothing otherwise had ever entered their minds—would be easy.

Swathed in their nylon cocoons, they were constantly aware of the falling snow, for it would build up on the tent sacks and eventually press down on their faces, needing every so often a strenuous shove to push it off. Towards midnight everyone was sunk in semi-dozes when Jack became aware of not having had pressure on his face for some length of time.

"Jesus, has a miracle happened?" he muttered to himself. Struggling his shoulders out of his sleeping bag he fumbled silk glovedly for the tent sac zip. The sheer coldness of the air tightened his features but his eyes happily gulped the bewildering impressions. The scenario was Tolkienesque. Cloud layers were splintering open, leaving star-filled gaps with moon tinted edges, a background to the white fingered Chamonix Aiguilles.

"Bloody fantastic," he gasped "John, John, wake up. The bastard's stopped. The stars are coming out."

John fumbled his head through the entrance. "Mother, oh Mother, I thought it was never going to happen. Do you think it's permanent?"

"Yeah. This one's breaking up at last and there's nothing forecast behind: we should be all right for a bit. We should start around 4 so we're completely ready at first light. I'll try to raise Chamonix at 1."

The wind was not strong, only infinitely bitter. During Alpine storms the temperature does not get outrageously low but often immediately afterwards during the reestablishment of a fine spell the isotherm drops way down and can provide extreme climbing conditions. From their icy airy perch they watched the clouds keep on breaking until a three quarter moon burst into view, giving an almost daylight panorama in the light reflected from the shimmering white landscape.

At 1 a.m. the dozing sergeant who had taken over the night watch from the Chief of Police, established himself on a comfortable chair in front of the radio, had his dreams of large breasts and welcoming thighs blown to oblivion by a violent crackling of static from the receiver. A ghostly voice filled the room.

"Jorasses to Chamonix. Jorasses to Chamonix. Does anyone read me?"

Grabbing the microphone he answered in French, for he
had been briefed that Jack spoke it fluently.

"Receiving you loud and clear. Go ahead."

"The storm's breaking up. I'd like to speak to the Chief of
Police and rescue at 6 a.m. What's the weather doing in
Chamonix?"

"Message understood. Hold!"

Rushing to the window the sergeant blinked into the broad
moonlight.

CHAPTER 14

WINCH JOB

While the four on the wall grabbed three hours' precious rest, telephones were ringing in darkened apartments all over Chamonix. By 5.30 police, guides, pilots and winchmen were shivering at the Gendarmerie, apprehensive yet excited at the thought of the day's activity. They stood gazing for a few moments at the sharp outlines of the Aiguilles in the bright moonlight, before trooping into the radio room to drink coffee and await the call from the wall.

There the weather was equally cold and good but conditions were by no means ideal. As Jack stuck his head out fifteen minutes before call time he could hardly make out if it was clear or not. The aftermath of the storm had set in: the spindrift was coming off the wall in rivers and an occasional puff of wind would send some rattling round the tent.

"Are you awake, John?"

"Yeah. What's happening?"

"The goddam spindrift's almost as bad as the storm was. We're still going to have to wait a few hours till most of it sloughs off. The rotor blades of a chopper would create a bloody maelstrom and it'd be just as dangerous as flying in a storm."

"O.K., bugger it. But shall I start getting Pat ready? It'll take some time."

"Sure. I'll just get on the air and then stand by."

When Jack's voice broke through once again into the crowded room Maurice took the communication.

"Yes, loud and clear, Jack. How are things?"

"Good morning, Maurice. Our weather's fine but the spindrift's very bad. Impossible rescue conditions until it drops. What are you doing?"

"We'll take off at first light to have a general look. We'll stay open all the time here so you can come in whenever you want. Please tell us immediately if conditions improve: we can relay back from here to the pilot."

"Roger, Maurice. At least the wind's moderate. I'd guess we might have a chance of some action around noon but will stand by. Any more for us?"

"One thing: what's the condition of the two climbers?"

"As reasonable as can be expected. Both conscious."

"Read you. Wait a minute."

After a quick talk with Bertrand, Dupré whispered: "Ask them if they want to be evacuated as well, if it's possible."

Maurice smiled. "I doubt that, but I'll ask."

Jack's answer seemed to fill the room.

"Negative. I repeat: negative. We appreciate the offer but will evacuate ourselves."

"Read you, Jack. It's what I expected. Out from us and standing by."

Jack signed off and Maurice turned to find a discussion going on.

"Last night Louis, Yves, Ronald and I talked it over," Bertrand was saying, "and our plan, provided you're all in agreement—especially Maurice and Pierre— is to fly in first, even with spindrift on the wall. I'd like to take a close look and then come back and report. Louis can go look for himself afterwards. If it's feasible we might have a go in one after the other." He stopped and looked at the others. Maurice and Pierre both nodded.

"When do you want to take off?"

"First light. 8 a.m. O.K.?"

"O.K."

Dupré interrupted: "You're probably going to be attacked by the press: They'll be hanging around all day. But just say no comment and refer them to me."

"O.K., Chief, gladly," grinned the pilots in unison. Cressier, a little more seriously, asked:

"What about air space? Do you think they'll start hiring planes to try to take pictures? Could be dangerous for us."

"I'm sure they will and unfortunately there's not much I can do about it. They can't get a helicopter because the nearest private company is in Grenoble and they rely on me for landing permission in this area. But I don't rule the air:

there's nothing to stop them hiring a private plane and buzzing around. I can appeal to their better instincts but it doesn't always work. We'll just have to play it by ear."

After coffee, omelettes and rolls, a large breakfast by French standards, the pilots went out to the landing pad to check their machines. Alouette is French for lark, but there is nothing particularly bird-like in the looks of the Alouette 3. A squat bulbous nose rests on three ski-type skids running into a long tail equipped with a rotor blade and stabilar. Three rotor blades and the powerful jet turbine motor cap the perspex cabin. Under ideal conditions it has a flying time of nearly three hours, a top speed of 200 k.p.h., and can carry six passengers or two stretched out. For wall rescues it is equipped with a winch and cable which at maximum can be dropped 25 metres and carry a load of 175 kg.

If the injured person is immobilised the rescuer carries a portable stretcher on his back and eventually fixes the victim to it while the pilot takes the helicopter out from the wall. As well as being dangerous for him, staying close can make the rotor blades cause stonefall or whirlwinds of fresh snow, endangering those on the wall. On receiving the thumbs up signal from the guide he comes back, cable ready to take off the victim. In an emergency he would fly straight to hospital and come back for the guide, who always carries a rucsac with bivouac gear in case he is stranded for a while.

On this occasion the pilots' tentative plan was to fly in one after the other, dropping only Maurice on to the wall. Before flying into the face they planned to set up a temporary command post on the Leschaux glacier manned by the other four guides, who were to be dropped on the rescue flight complete with tent, radios, food and spare clothing.

Steve, Walter and Susie arrived in the midst of the action and were put into the picture by Maurice, to whom Walter mentioned an idea they had agreed upon during the night:

"I think Steve and I will ski down the Vallée Blanche and walk up to the foot of the wall with John and Jack's skis and spare food and gaz and stay in the ice cave until they come down. They're going to be pretty wiped out."

Maurice pondered. "Good idea, but wait a minute: I've a better one." He went over to the two pilots and muttered a few words. They grinned and nodded. Maurice sauntered back smiling.

"Better still, Louis has agreed to drop you on the Leschaux so that you can make up your minds what to do when you see what's happened."

Both Steve and Walter broke into big grins. "Fantastic. Merci. It'll be great to be close to the scene.

Inside the building Dupré's day was starting in the fashion he had expected. In the last hour he had taken two calls from London, one from Glasgow, one from Edinburgh, two from Paris, one from Lausanne and two from Geneva as well as from two local reporters. To each he had given the same answer: that reconnaissance flights were being made with a view to possible evacuation from the wall and that there would be no further news until midday. Instructing his secretary to carry on, he hurried out to the tarmac as the first streaks of dawn turned the sky from deep black to promising blue.

But there was no peace for him: parked there were the newly arrived cars of the two local reporters, drawn like magnets by the whine of an engine starting. To their deluge of questions he restated what he had told them over the phone, but it was not enough for the two pressmen.

"Who's going to land on the wall?"

"What happens if you can't pick them up?"

The Chief waved them away, friendly but non-commital.

"We'll face those eventualities if and when they happen. At the moment there's nothing more to say until Bertrand comes back. I suggest you go back to your offices and I'll have someone keep you up to date."

Mureau had been reporting climbing for years and knew the Chief's ways.

"O.K., Chief. Do you mind if I just take some pictures of the take-off, then I'll leave you in peace?"

"Go ahead," invited Dupré, "but stay out of range. The boys are busy."

Jules Blanc of the Tribune was not so phlegmatic. Young and new to the region, he thought they should be allowed to sit in on the radio calls and hear everything first hand. The Chief's off-hand manner annoyed him.

"Complacent bastard," he muttered to his rival.

Mureau laughed. "That's just his attitude. We'll get the goods when he wants and not before. He always comes across in the end." Teasing the eager Blanc, he added: "Why don't you put your skis on and go and have a look for yourself?"

But Blanc did not react to his humour. Instead a new idea was creeping into his head.

A first-hand picture. He would hire a plane and fly close in to the wall and get some pictures of the section.

Mureau could almost read what he was thinking. "It's not worth the time or trouble hiring a plane. These guys"— indicating the pilots with a jerk of his thumb—"don't like planes messing about when they're flying rescues and all the local companies are in so thick with them they won't fly."

Blanc's mind was racing. He had just had what he thought to be a brilliant idea but, keeping a deadpan face, he pretended to acknowledge defeat.

"Suppose you're right. They're a cliquey lot of sods. I think I'll go and file this information."

He strolled nonchalantly to his car. But once in, he gunned the Citreon Diane away as fast as its feeble engine would carry him towards his telephone. He had a friend in Annecy who had recently qualified for mountain flying and had his own plane. If he paid all expenses, Blanc was sure Boursier would come just for the hell of it.

His phone call was successful, for Boursier had heard of the impending rescue on the radio. Blanc infected him with enthusiasm, telling him excitedly how they would get fantastic pictures and scoop the world. They arranged to meet at Megève, the nearest landing strip, two hours later.

On the face of it there was not much activity, only the painful ritual of cooking in cramped and freezing conditions. As the cold stark dawn gained ground both the injured men sank into depression as the realisation of what had happened came through to them for the first time. John's slightest movement jarred Craig's leg, causing him to cry out, and there was no way John could avoid him in the desperate closeness of the tent sack.

But as the first hot drinks started to run through their bodies, wills became stronger and they began to talk more hopefully. It had taken nearly three-and-a-half painful hours for John to wake up fully, cook and get Craig in a position to be moved.

When Jack came on the air at 8 o'clock, reporting continued spindrift, the Gendarmerie was a hive of activity. Bertrand, lost in concentration already, was warming the Alouette's engines under the gaze of a rubbernecked crowd eager for drama, while gendarmes shouted and the phone rang incessantly. Dupré was a busy man.

Circling to gain height, Bertrand was soon out of the Chamonix Valley and in a few minutes was coming in high from the Aiguilles and making a straight cut up the Leschaux glacier.

The four on the wall could hear the unmistakable sound as he approached and their mood changed suddenly from the damp pessimism of the early hours to cautious optimism. Jack hoped that the pilot would not have to make a negative decision as it would be psychologically damaging to the patients' condition to have their hopes raised and dashed again.

They did not have to land on the Leschaux. Coming in fast Bertrand hovered just above the snow and the two guides Monder and Lionel jumped out on to the crevasse free glacier, laughing as they disappeared up to their waists in snow. Maurice threw their equipment out and in a few seconds Bertrand was off again, leaving them with a huge blast of powder snow from the rotors as he began his wide circling to gain height for the run into the face.

"*Merde*," he swore, "there sure is a lot of snow coming down. Still, let's have a look."

Slowly they circled into the huge mass of the wall until all that was immediately visible was rock and ice. Seen from the helicopter the face looked appallingly difficult. As a non-mountaineer, Bertrand could never quite understand peoples' urges to go into such hostile territory. Closer and closer the fragile machine powered into the bowl.

"There they are," Maurice pointed. They could see the red tent sacs plainly against the snow and two figures, Jack and John, standing on the ledge. Bertrand could pick out the features clearly and made his decision fast, conveying it to the others over the intercom.

"I'm going out and round to come in from the Central Couloir side, then I'll take her slowly up. But if we disturb too much snow I'll have to pull out fast."

Maurice had an idea. "Can you put me out on the winch? If you can hold it I'd like to look at the area."

Souchard indicated that this was O.K., so Maurice clipped on to the karabiner at the end of the winch and sat on the edge, feet dangling over a thousand metres of space, eyes watering, and waited for Bertrand to go in. There was no more talk between them now: each was concentrating wholly on his own task.

Slowly, delicately, Bertrand brought the machine into the great bowl of the wall and there, right in front of Maurice, was the straight drop of the ice couloir, looking absolutely vertical from his position. The machine crept up closer and closer till they were only fifty metres from the wall.

Maurice broke the silence: "I see it," he pointed to the section above the couloir. Bertrand came closer and the rotor blades' wind began stirring great gusts of powder from the wall.

"I can hold it here," muttered Bertrand, "just above and out from the top of the couloir."

"O.K., let me down." Maurice tapped the winchman's shoulder, gave him the thumbs-up sign and stepped out.

The first moments of going down on the wire are the worst as the total exposure has its effect. Maurice had made this movement countless times but always had a moment or two wondering about the strength of the wire before his faith returned.

Pirouetting gently over the morasse of ice and rock, he quickly made up his mind after five metres and signalled for Souchard to bring him up. Bertrand wasted no time: bringing the nose round to point towards the Leschaux Glacier he blasted off towards the sunshine as Maurice was still being winched in.

Sprawling on the floor, Maurice unclipped, relieved to be out of the air, and shoved the earphones over his head.

"It's possible from my angle," he gasped, breathing hard.

Bertrand turned and gave him a grin. "I think I can do it, but do me a favour, Maurice: don't hang about."

Maurice laughed. "Just don't forget about me."

Bertrand carried on more seriously: "I think we should wait a couple of hours to let some of the snow come down. I'd hate to get blinded when I was sitting there but I couldn't feel any really bad currents, so we should be all right."

Five minutes later they were down in Chamonix, rushing through the questioning crowd into the safety of the Gendarmerie. Once they were safely behind doors wide grins burst on to everyone's faces when they heard the news. They rushed up to the control room. The operator waved a beckoning hand: "McDonald has just been on and is staying open."

Dupré whispered to Maurice: "You'd better tell him the good news."

On the wall front they had watched wide-eyed the manoeuvres of the helicopter. Then came anxious questions from Craig and Anderson. Jack could only mumble, "Wait, see and hope."

The atmosphere was tense as Maurice came through. "Do you read me, Jack?"

"Loud and clear, Maurice. What do you think?"

"Positive Jack, repeat positive. We think we can do it. Can you start evacuation and let us know when you are in position? We're standing by to fly."

"Fantastic, Maurice. We'll start immediately. Out from us."

Jack and John strapped on their crampons ready to climb again. "Did you hear that fellow?" Jack asked the two injured. "If Bertrand thinks he can get you off there's a bloody good chance that he will. John, could you abseil down to the top of the couloir, excavate as much of a stance as you can, put in some anchor pitons, and come back up and help lower me down with Pat? I'll do the same thing as yesterday: get him on my back."

"O.K. Fine by me," said John. "How do you feel, Pat?"

"Bloody awful, but a lot more optimistic after seeing the helicopter."

Anderson broke in. "We're going to owe you guys our lives, you know."

"Save all that until you're safe in Chamonix," Jack cut in abruptly. "There's still a hell of a lot of hard work to be done. Gerry, can you keep some hot drinks going while we're working?"

"Fine. As long as I don't move my head it's bearable."

Knowing that the slightest knock could be very dangerous John had lent Anderson his hard hat. Checking the rest of the equipment he grabbed a bunch of pitons and abseiled down to the edge of the couloir, feeling a great relief at being able to stretch and move about at random.

The spindrift had slackened considerably. After such a heavy drop of snow the accumulation becomes so great that it slides off almost as soon as it lands, and as the wind had nearly died the conditions were becoming close to ideal for a pick up; but if any wind, however slight, sprang up there could be a whole new difficult perspective to things.

As John was hacking out a stance and placing pitons they heard the sound of a helicopter heading up the Leschaux and could see more figures hopping off at the same point as the other guides had been dropped. It was Cressier, making a fast trip to get the camp established on the glacier before he too climbed up to have a look at the wall. He was travelling with just his winchman, Soumils, for they had changed their ideas in order to do things as fast as possible.

The latest plan was for Maurice to be dropped by Bertrand, who would circle back round, pick up Craig and drop him on the glacier. Cressier, following him in, would lift Anderson off, drop down to pick up Craig and fly them both to hospital while Bertrand picked up Maurice and evacuated the mountain. It was a fine-edged plan which, given nothing going wrong, could have the whole rescue done within half an hour.

John hung on to his pitons as the wind of the rotor blades blasted powder into his face. Cressier brought the machine up level with him but stayed about fifty metres out before turning down and curving steeply to the valley.

In the Gendarmerie the phone calls were stepping up: the Chief told his secretary to release a statement that they would be attempting a pick-up around noon, conditions permitting, but that he himself was not available for comment.

From Geneva, the freelance correspondents of many of the major English dailies, and the *New York Herald Tribune*, hustled over to Chamonix to join the crowd of locals around the perimeter of the landing pad watching eagerly as the pilots came and went.

At Megève airport, Jules Blanc of the Tribune anxiously waited for his wife, watching the helicopters in Chamonix, to send him the word that would set him and his pilot friend airborne. On hearing the news from the Gendarmerie, he slapped Boursier on the back.

"Incredible. If we take off when they do we can be right on the spot and get pictures of the pick-up from the wall."

Boursier was no less keen. He had invested in his plane to catch some of the profitable Air Taxi business, and he knew that if he got known to the newspapers as one who was not afraid to take a few risks a good deal of work could come his way. He was aware of the helicopter pilots' dislike of having anyone in the air at the same time as them, but thought their strictures over-cautious: he reckoned he would not be interfering with what was going on as he could not get as close to the wall as they.

Cheerfully they checked the plan over.

On the Leschaux glacier the guides and Steve and Walter had a large area stamped out and a tent pitched, coffee brewing and the binoculars set to watch Jack preparing to take Craig on his back and start the descent.

John jumared back up the rope to the bivouac, and Jack picked up the radio.

"Ready to start lowering."

"Roger," Dupré returned. "Tell us when you have him down and we'll start flying."

"Roger. Out for now."

It was nearly forty metres down to the other ledge and John had left the rope closely in place. Jack wanted to control himself standing up in the normal abseil position while John had him on a tight safety rope.

Carefully they lifted Craig out of the tent sac, fully clothed but with his injured leg wrapped in a down inner boot and jacket to keep it warm and loose. His face was white, drawn and grey with pain but his morale still high. He obeyed their instructions implicitly. Jack knelt down and John slowly lifted him round until he could be clipped on to Jack's harness. From there his leg was hanging straight over the edge in its down-wrapped splint so that it would not bump into anything.

"Ready Pat," said John.

"O.K., O.K."

Pulling on a piton Jack slowly stood up, found his balance while John held him tight on the rope, and stepped back off the ledge. The strain as always was terrible on his legs and the last thing he wanted was to swing sideways and crash Craig into unthought of agony against the wall. But his balance held up and in fifteen minutes he was signalling his arrival on the ledge and kneeling to take the strain from his legs. John immediately abseiled down the fixed safety rope and together they laid Craig on the ledge.

"O.K., Pat."

"Fine, you guys. You're just fantastic."

Jack rested for a few moments. "Let's get Gerry down now. I don't think we'll have to carry him: I can just lower him down if you guide him, John."

"O.K."

In another thirty minutes they were all on the lower stance and Jack was radioing to Chamonix.

"Action stations."

"Roger," said the Chief, and rushed to the window to give the thumbs up to Bertrand who was already waiting with his engine warmed up, ready to go.

He came back to Jack. "Taking off now."

"Waiting. Out from the wall."

The airplane from Megève was airborne five minutes later as the telephone message came through from Chamonix. In another five they would be over the Jorasses, hopefully in a good position to catch most of the action, estimating that Bertrand would have another look round before going in.

Bertrand took off, winging down the Chamonix Valley with Cressier a few seconds behind him. Flying conditions were as good as they could be as they climbed slowly up the Mer de Glace. Cressier held back from the wall, flying up to the Talefre Glacier side while Bertrand went in.

Circling up again Bertrand was soon at the level of the four waiting figures and this time he didn't hesitate. Checking the conditions with a swift glance he went straight in until he was about twenty metres above the climbers. Maurice was ready as he slowly held the Alouette there, the wall appearing huge and frightening, only a few metres away. Then Maurice was spinning down on the winch, guided feet first by Jack on to the ledge. In seconds he had released himself from the cable and was being slapped on the shoulder by Jack as he gave the thumbs up and Betrand pulled steeply and quickly away.

They muttered a few words and grinned happily. Maurice, looking cool and fresh and unruffled, stared into the haunted frost-burned faces of the climbers marked by their days on the wall. But there was no time for chatter; the helicopter was turning fast and Bertrand was beginning the climb up again.

"I didn't bring a stretcher," Maurice shouted above the noise. "We thought it would be quicker but there's one waiting down on the camp on the Leschaux."

As the nose of the helicopter turned towards the wall again the winch wire came snaking down. In a few seconds Maurice had it clipped to the harness he had put round Craig's shoulders. Thumbs up again. The winch tightened and with a sharp cry of pain Craig was off and Bertrand was heading out, swinging victim and machine from the wall towards the sunlit glacier below.

Unnoticed because of the noise of the helicopter, a small red plane suddenly flew across the front of the wall a good way out but on the level of the climbers. Bertrand swore violently as he saw it just above his line of vision, and grabbed the radio.

"Chief. Part of the mission successful but there's a plane in the area. Can you locate and get the bastard out of here?"

The Chief cursed too. "O.K., will try." But his attempts met with no success. The pair in the plane had turned off the radio because they knew there could be attempts to warn them off.

Blanc turned excitedly to the pilot. "Fantastic, I got some good telephoto shots but can you get in any closer?"

Boursier nodded. "Next time they go in I'll fly right past just outside the helicopter. How does that sound?"

"Great. Just great. We could have the pictures of the century."

Cressier had wasted no time and was making his approach in turn. The same profound steadiness and complete calmness was apparent as he approached slowly and brought his machine level with the group on the wall. There he waited for a few seconds, testing and checking conditions, before he too began to draw in with the winch wire snaking down. Just as it reached the ledge, Boursier came right round, his tiny Cessna in the arc of the Jorasses, flying as slowly as he could so that Blanc could take his pictures. Control seemed straight forward and he risked a glance towards the wall, but suddenly there was a tremendous lurch as the plane hit an air pocket and dropped like a stone.

Boursier gave a horrified yell. "I can't hold her."

They were his last words. In front of the horrified eyes of the people on the wall the plane flew straight into the buttress of the Walker Spur and disintegrated with a terrible explosion.

Sick throughout his whole body Maurice mechanically carried out the motions of attaching a retching Anderson to the wire and gave the thumbs up to Cressier who with icy calm flew out from the wall down towards the glacier.

"*Nom de Dieu,*" exclaimed Maurice quietly. "They're kaput."

As Bertrand came wheeling in again he turned to Jack. "Are you sure you don't want to be taken off? The conditions are perfect."

Jack looked at John, who shook his head. "No, we'll get out ourselves, you'd better go and see if there's anything left of those poor bastards."

Maurice shook his head. "There's no hope but we'll have a look anyway," and as Bertrand closed in again he shook both their hands.

"Good luck," and then he too was gone. Swinging dramatically at the end of the wire leaving Jack and John slightly stunned and disbelieving as the silence closed in on them.

Everything had happened so quickly that it seemed as if they had always been alone on the mountain. Yet in the past fifteen minutes one of the smoothest and most successful mountain rescues yet attempted had been successfully completed. But the pleasure had already a bitter feeling in the hearts of the rescuers for they knew that they would have to turn back into the wall and look for dead bodies in the wreckage strewn across the glacier at the foot of the wall.

For the pilot, winchman and guide there is always an urge which keeps them going even when conditions are very difficult if they are pulling out victims who are still alive. It is one of the built-in satisfactions of the job that no matter how stupid people have been in getting into the situation that calls for rescue, the helicopter team can at least give them another chance in life by the careful use of their technical skills and fine sense of calculated risk-taking. But looking for dead bodies is a totally different matter. The pilot often feels disinclined to push things and the atmosphere in the 'plane can become dull and leaden, workaday, especially when you are stuffing what used to be people into sacks and hauling them down.

Unfortunately dead bodies have to be collected as well as live ones. In many instances insurance companies demand a body before they will pay a life policy, so the pilots in a way are flying for the dependents' sakes. It never makes the job any more pleasant.

CHAPTER 15

SUCCESS

Jack and John jumared back up to the bivouac site and John got out the stove. They sat on the ledge surveying the beautiful day. There was still a lot of snow around but most of it had sloughed off. Regarding the wall above contemplatively while John manoeuvred the stove Jack found his thoughts expanding outwards again.

For the last two days they had been locked into a rigid pattern of carrying out and organising the rescue operation. His only thoughts had been to get it done successfully and prepare their own evacuation. But as he sat in the sun nearly a thousand metres up that great wall another idea began to make its presence felt.

"How do you feel, John?"

John looked at him questioningly. "A bit bewildered by the suddenness of it all. I almost feel that Craig and Anderson are still in the tent sacs. But otherwise I'm fine." He stirred the melting ice with a piton. "When do you think we should start down?"

Jack looked down towards the Aiguilles and was silent for a moment. "How do you feel about continuing?"

John turned to face him sharply, almost knocking over the tea. "Jesus Christ, Jack. What an idea. But shit why the hell not? I've been so preoccupied with getting those two down and off the wall that I'd almost forgotten that the summit of Jorasses existed. Do you feel like it?"

"Yeah, I do. There's absolutely no reason why we shouldn't carry on. We still have supplies. Neither of us are particularly wiped out. I know people will call us callous bastards after everything that's happened, but if we went down we'd only want to come back again. Now we're in a good position and the weather looks good too." He gazed down towards the snow covered Aiguilles glistening in the sun. "It's shorter up than down."

"O.K., " said John. "Let's give it a try. We still have the fixed rope up to Anderson's stance and I reckon we can get at least one more rope length done today. Back down here for the night then zap onwards tomorrow?"

Jack was impressed by the adaptability of John's mind. "Can't find any fault with that but we'd better see if we can raise anyone on the radio to tell them our plans."

"Chamonix might still be switched on: let's try anyway."

"Jorasses to Chamonix, come in please. Jorasses to Chamonix."

Dupré and Cressier were in the control room, speculating on the plane crash victims, when Jack's voice came on the wire loud and clear. Briefly he told Dupré their plans.

The Chief thought for a minute, then replied: "I think you are crazy but, well, good luck. Your friends are on the Leschaux glacier. Do you want to contact them?"

"Yeah. Can you arrange for them to call us at 6 p.m. tonight?"

Cressier signalled to Dupré that he wanted to speak.

"This is Cressier. Do you read me, McDonald?"

"Yes, Louis, reading you. That was fantastic flying this afternoon."

"Merci. Merci. I only wanted to say we'll keep an eye on you. If you succeed we'll pick you up from the top."

Jack thought for a moment, reflected that it was slightly against his principles, but decided he could not turn down what was obviously meant as a super friendly gesture. "That's an offer we can't refuse. Thank you. How are Anderson and Craig?"

"Both are in the hospital and in good shape."

"Do you know who the plane crash victims were?"

Dupré took over: "No, but we're working on it. Do you have anything more?"

"No. Out from the Jorasses."

"Out from Chamonix. Good luck."

He turned to Cressier: "I've spent twenty years of my life in Chamonix, working with mountaineers a lot of the time; but sometimes I wonder if I'll ever understand them. I'd have been headed for the quickest way down to a good meal and a warm bed. Wouldn't you?"

Cressier nodded. "Personally yes, but working with them daily I've come to understand them a little better than I did when I started. Sometimes I'll have a guide working a rescue stint with me from Monday to Saturday; but does he go home and spend Sunday with his wife and kids? No. He's off climbing for his own sake. I think someone like McDonald would work it out clinically. I don't know his partner so well, but Jack, from what I've gathered, would do the rescue work and then take a long look at himself. If he reckoned he'd tired himself out he'd come down. But if he was feeling in good shape then he'd want to press on. After all, that's why he was here in the first place."

Dupré eyed the pilot speculatively. It was a long and philosophical speech for one who usually restricted himself to practical terms about rescues and the machine he flew. But his reflections were cut short by the arrival of a sergeant clutching a piece of paper.

"You're not going to like this, Sir. A Cessna from Annecy took off shortly before midday from Megève, with Jules Blanc of the Tribune as solo passenger, heading for the Mont Blanc range. There has been radio silence ever since."

"Merde!" swore Dupré, and buried his head in his hands.

When Bertrand came through half an hour later his fears were confirmed.

"I'm on the Leschaux, Chief. I dropped Maurice and Monder on the Glacier at the foot of the Walker and they've just called me. There's not much left of the plane, but they've found a wallet. Jules Blanc." The message was conveyed in the cold factual tone of one who had seen much death. "Can Cressier come and help evacuate?"

"Roger," said Dupré. "Oh, one more thing. Will you tell McDonald's friends that they're continuing with the climb and would like a call at 1800 hours?"

They could almost hear Bertrand whistle. "I sure will, Chief. What a pair." There was a pause. "Maybe I can pick them up from the top."

Dupré laughed. "You can fight that one out with Cressier, who's already offered; but as far as I'm concerned you'll be on a routine flight and happen to see them, and do it for the training. That way the taxpayers can't complain."

He signed off and turned to Cressier, his face saddening. "Well, I'd better face Mme Blanc and then the press."

"Right, Chief," replied Cressier, pausing with his hand on the door. "You know, they say our job's dangerous, but I'd rather be up there flying around in no matter what kind of conditions than have to handle the type of job you have down here. Well, I'm off."

As they prepared to start climbing John and Jack watched the helicopters swoop in and out collecting their various loads.

Bertrand picked up the lifeless bundles which had been Blanc and Boursier, attached them to a rescue bag and winged his way down towards the Chamonix mortuary. Cressier crossed his flight and came straight in to pick up Maurice and Monder, who were patiently waiting, discussing the last few eventful hours. They did not know that John and Jack were going to continue climbing and found out to their great surprise when they were winched up a few minutes later.

Shall we go in and take a last look?" said Cressier. "I'll stay well out but you can see what the climbing's like at least."

"Sure," nodded Maurice. "I can take some pictures of the situation for the record."

Pulling back up into the amphitheatre they were able to see and photograph the two tiny figures, one of whom had already started to move up the fixed rope from the stance.

Maurice gestured to the winchman. "Do you have the loudhailer?"

"Sure," replied Souchard, handing it over.

"Good luck," echoed out from the helicopter. They could see both figures give a one-handed wave, then Cressier was blasting out from the wall, leaving them once again alone with the mountain. They zoomed low over the Leschaux glacier where Steve and Walter were looking across towards the hut and descended reluctantly towards Chamonix, the press, the television and the official report filing which they knew would fill the rest of their day.

Jack and John jumared up the ropes to Anderson's ledge

and sat there for a few minutes quietly organising the equipment, savouring the silence and getting ready to switch their minds to the actual business of climbing once again.

"Well, I reckon it's my turn," murmured John, "after your efforts on the first pitch. It looks hard enough but at least I have daylight and good weather. Might at least get a rest on what's left of the flake that Craig pulled off. Should be solid enough now."

"Yeah," agreed Jack, "if you can get to the roof I can clean it. Should give us a good start in the morning."

"Feels pretty good sitting here. There must be all hell going on down in Chamonix."

"Jesus, yes. I'm ready to move. You O.K.?"

"Yeah, fine."

John felt clumsy at first on the delicate friable rock held together by frost. But slowly the blood began to flow once again at a normal rate in his limbs, not feeling like sluggish cold water as it often did in winter. The climbing was hard and needed silk gloves to find and clean out what small holds there were. Mainly he resorted to artificial climbing to save time but the pitons he placed were often tied off short. Gladly he reached the one which had stopped Craig's fall and clipped into it for a rest, relaxing for a moment as its solidity had been well proven.

Off to the west an afternoon tinge was coming over the sky and the sun dropped past the Aiguilles and down to the end of the Chamonix Valley. Unaware that the eyes and ears of many people throughout the world were fixed on them as their rope ran steadily through Jack's hands, John continued breaking the afternoon silence with the scrape of crampons, the rattle of pitons and occasional sharp exhalation of breath after a particularly savage lunge. There is nothing delicate and floating about winter climbing. Cocooned in warm clothing, gloves and large double boots your upwards movement seems to consist of a series of contemplated crampon-scraping lunges, with short rests in between, bearing very little relation to the fluidity of movement that you can attain on summer rock. The nailing got thinner as John neared the roof but by means of a series of tied off knife blades he found himself eventually securing the rope for Jack on a one foothold ledge and bending his head backwards to peer at the roof.

A jagged crack line winged out horizontally for ten metres, looking as if it would take large size pitons. It reminded John very much of the roof on his solo new route far away on Aonach Dubh, but this time he had a partner. Anyway it was Jack's turn to lead.

As the sun began to take its dying dip for the day Jack arrived in a cluster of pitons and slings and both looked at the foreshortened way ahead.

"Looks O.K.," said Jack. "Maybe you can use one of my cameras and get some pictures. Could be far out."

"Sure, I'll try," laughed John, "but we may as well get back down to the bivouac. I'm ready to eat."

"Me too." Clipping on to the figure of eight Jack slid down the rope and as the last patch of light left the sky both were once again in their tent sacs, luxuriating in the extra space and leisure now that they were alone.

The radio conversation that night with the trio in the Leschaux was light hearted and warm. It was the first time they had talked together since the heavily weighted morning when Walter and Susie had set off in the dark and storm from the Leschaux for Chamonix. At the success of the rescue everyone felt slightly euphoric, for it had involved highly technical and often brilliant work on the part of those involved and there would have been a great personal sense of loss if any fatal accident had befallen anyone actively concerned, whether rescuer or victim. Jack or John, despite their mental hardness would have found it very difficult to contemplate a continuation of the route and the Chamonix people would probably have urged them to come down. But the plane crash, although it had affected them, had something of the impact of a film scene. It had been a visual flash, and somehow it seemed removed from the realms of their immediate feelings.

With the news of a good weather forecast for the next two or three days they both fell into a dreamless sleep. Peace and limited human activity reigned once again on the Grandes Jorasses.

Down in Chamonix it was a different story, and by no means as calm and happy a one. Jeanique Blanc was taking the news of her husband's death badly, and there was a considerable press contingent clamouring for a story. The rescue teams had almost had to fight their way from the machines into the Gendarmerie. Dupré had called a press conference, and shortly before it the news of the plane crash broke, so it was a very interested and attentive audience who waited as Dupré gave them a resumé of what had happened. It made an excellent story and all was going relatively easy until one of the correspondents asked casually, "When do you expect McDonald and Dunlop to be down?"

Maurice's answer, "They're continuing the climb," made everyone sit up. Dupré could foresee a flood of telephone calls to the private plane companies asking for flights round the Jorasses. It was the last thing the journalists had expected. But then the nasty questions started:

"They must be pretty callous characters to be able to continue climbing after the rescue and the plane crash."

"What happens if they have an accident?"

"Don't they think of you guys?"

"What about the taxpayers who are paying for these expensive rescues?"

Dupré waited until the shouts had died down. "I don't see any callousness involved at all. These climbers had their climb interrupted by the accident, and carrying out their magnificent part of the rescue action undoubtedly saved the lives of the two injured, and incidentally saved the taxpayers the cost of a much vaster and more complex rescue operation. Concerning their reaction to the plane crash, it should be borne in mind that they didn't know the victims and even so the fact that they have elected to climb up instead of down in no way reflects their sense of sorrow."

The room was quiet now as he continued. "We all feel a great sense of bereavement at the loss of the two in the plane but it should be remembered that they were going against our helicopter rescue policy in flying round the scene of an accident whilst helicopters were in the air. Please remember this if you want to hire planes to take pictures tomorrow and call me first as we shall be making routine flights. As far as a rescue of the two on the wall is concerned; I don't think they'll need it. But if they do happen to get into trouble they will be treated exactly like any other mountaineers—i.e. we shall attempt a rescue. That is what the rescue service is for and it is a service like any other public service—fire, ambulance and so on—available for anyone. Now, any more questions?"

The pressmen were rather stunned by this vehement assertion but Dupré knew he had only gained a temporary respite till they started looking for more headlines. They had an excellent story but in an attempt to hold public interest a few would probably hang on the question of whether climbers should continue after an accident or not.

It was a controversial issue in climbing and many major expeditions had aborted after an accident because it was considered the ethically correct way of showing their grief. But recently there had been an increasing tendency for climbers to continue ascents as it was reckoned that it showed no disrespect to the accident victims. Yet in public circles the feeling was still very much that it was hard-hearted and callous to continue after accidents, especially fatal ones, and journalists often seized the chance to stir up controversy whenever they could. Dupré was sure that, when the climbing was actually taking place, certain papers would raise the ethical considerations of whether they were right in opting to continue.

After the journalists had trooped out Dupré gave a shrug and a sigh and invited the rescuers upstairs to his office. As they sprawled around relaxing he reached into one of his cupboards and brought out a bottle of Scotch and several glasses.

"Now, let's hear the real story," he said with a smile.

John and Jack started their breakfast preparation early, feeling well rested by the night's sleep and the fact that they had almost been able to stretch out fully in their individual hammocks. They ate as much as they could stuff in, together with a lot of liquid. The morning was sharp, cold and clear, with the black fading out into blue as they finally packed up their rucsacs happy to be able to continue and move within the realms of their own wishes unhampered by the needs of others. Soon they were swinging from pitons on the tiny stance beneath the roof and hauling up the ropes and sacs prior to attacking what was undoubtedly the major obstacle to upward progress.

The ice pitons were stowed away in a rucsac and the full assortment of rock pitons brought out. Jack slung a bunch of thirty various sizes of pin, carefully racked three to a karabiner, round his shoulder, adding some forty karabiners racked in pairs and finally various assorted slings, pitons and aid slings. Taking his camera from around his neck he handed it to John with a smile.

"It's all set. Just point it and keep your gloves away from the lens."

"O.K. chief."

"Ready?"

"Ready as I'll ever be."

Jack set off and for the next two hours he did not falter. The pitch demanded a wide diversity of pitons from knife blades going up to the roof to large bongs on the horizontal, backwards, upside down, swinging traverse but even though the placements were difficult he made no mistakes; it was straight patient all-demanding artificial climbing. John developed a pain in his neck muscles watching the gently swinging figure above him, conscious, as Jack was not, of the thousand metres of air that he was suspended over. But it was done without incident and the rope was anchored off so he could follow. There was a brief flash of the total wildness of the situation as he let the two sacs swing free on the spare rope so Jack could haul them over the top. Penduling and gyrating they swung out in a huge arc before Jack's upward pull took them out of sight. John hoped that none of the roof pitons would pull as he was denailing, or he would be in for a similar swing, but it was a day when the sun was shining on their efforts: an hour later he arrived breathing heavily, laden with pitons, above the roof. It was a tiny stance looking out and away across multitudes of peaks to the plains on the horizon, and it represented their total commitment to climbing out. Getting back down the roof could prove ultra difficult or even impossible, but the way ahead looked much easier. The crack opened out into a wide snowy chimney showing sunlight glistening on the summit crest of the Walker Spur only some two hundred and fifty metres above their heads.

"Good lead, Jack," muttered John when he had regained his breath and pointed upwards: "I hardly dare say it but looks as if we could bivouac somewhere close to the top tonight."

"Mm," nodded Jack hopefully, "maybe, but you never know with these chimneys. All we need is a couple of overhanging chockstones and we're slowed right down. But we should get a comfortable bivouac."

"Yeah," agreed John. "Anyway I'll get moving. That sunlight's beginning to have a lot of attraction. Can you stick some of this gear in a rucsac?" He pointed to a pile of pitons, "I won't be able to move free climbing with all of it."

All afternoon they made steady progress. Around four they heard a small airplane approaching, a sound which made their blood run cold after the experience of the day before. But this time the pilot, in a Pilatus Porter, stayed well out from the wall. Even so they could see the people clearly silhouetted and could imagine they heard the snap of the cameras. They were not wrong in their assumptions either: with Dupré's approval, four of the correspondents had got together and rented a plane from Megève.

The climbing proved difficult enough but they moved relatively quickly, and by nightfall were busy scraping out a commodious ledge beneath a chockstone a mere hundred metres from the summit.

There was no need to sling the hammocks: by radio call time they were sitting comfortably side by side in one tent sac, heads out in the high sharp night with the only sign of civilisation a faint winking light in the window of the Leschaux hut.

In the Chamonix hospital Dupré and Monder were paying a visit to Craig and Anderson. Craig was under heavy sedation, but Anderson, whose skull fracture was light, was able to talk lucidly. Slowly Dupré and Monder pieced together the story and became fully aware of the magnitude of the work that

Jack and John had done. Hearing first hand about the desperate conditions and the technical difficulty of the ground they whistled silently to themselves.

When Anderson asked after them and Monder told him about the continuation of the climb, he said simply:

"Well, now I know the difference between the very top league and people like myself."

Taking their leave, the pair walked out into the late Chamonix afternoon.

"At least he's appreciative," muttered Dupré.

"At the moment," replied Monder cynically. "I've seen it all before. In two months he'll have forgotten all about it and will be trying something else. I gathered from McDonald's friends that this pair were a special combination of blockheads. Accidents don't make permanent changes to characters like that: they only temporarily alter the pattern of their behaviour."

"Well, you're the climber. But if you're right I hope they keep off my patch of grass in the future," said Dupré. "And they can take the gentlemen of the press with them too."

The four journalists who had made the flight past the wall and seen the high position of the pair had already excitedly filed their stories, and as people sat down to supper that night the word was out around the world that the Jorasses rescuers were close to the summit. The 'disrespecters of death brigade' were gathering momentum and everyone was manoeuvring for the first exclusive interview with the pair when they got down. Next afternoon would see an influx of cars going through the Mont Blanc tunnel and round to Val Ferret on the Italian side, where the Jorasses descent comes out, to catch them.

In the radio room at the Gendarmerie Moncher and Dupré, with Maurice whom they had picked up en route, waited patiently for six o'clock. Listening before cutting in they heard the interchange between Walter and Jack—Walter hyper-enthusiastic,—Jack still cautious—and waited until they had finished before interrupting.

"Receiving you loud and clear, Chamonix," Jack crackled through.

"We've just heard of the fantastic progress. What do you

reckon your summit time should be?"

"Optimistically, mid to late morning."

"O.K. Jack, we'll have a look around. A routine check, you know? How are wall conditions?"

"Excellent: some wind but not strong, very cold but little spindrift. We'll look forward to seeing you."

"Fine. Out from Chamonix. Leschaux Hut, can you hear me?"

"Yes, Maurice, go ahead."

"Walter, I suggest you ski out early tomorrow morning and go straight to your chalet. We'll contact you with developments. It's a circus down here.

"Appreciate that advice Maurice. Will do. Out from Leschaux."

"Chamonix out."

Around 7 p.m. in Edinburgh Judy received a call from Charlie. They had been in constant communication since the story had broken.

"Have you heard the news?" said Charlie.

"Yes, it's fantastic."

"Well I'm on my way down tonight. I've reserved two places Edinburgh-London-Geneva 7.50 tomorrow. Are you coming?"

"You bet your bloody life I am. I'll make up the spare bed. They should get down in a couple of days."

"That's what I reckon but we'd do as well to get there anyway in case they go like race horses. See you."

"O.K. Till later."

In Paris Lucien was getting ready for the long drive to Chamonix.

In Leysin the girls in the Vagabond bar looked at each other.

"Well, I guess we'll be skiing Chamonix for the next couple of days."

On the Jorasses Jack and John were having a discussion on the ethics of the possible helicopter pick up in between large draughts of lemon tea, still unaware of the world's interest. Jack reckoned that the story bubble would burst with the end of the rescue. He knew that some people would be wanting their personal revelations but for once he miscalculated the amount of impact a climbing story would make on the world at large.

It was he who broached the subject.

"You know, John, it'd be a beautiful thing to be picked up from the top tomorrow, and I'd certainly welcome it, but somehow there's an old fashioned nag from my climbing conscience that wants to say: finish and descend on your own steam. At the same time I know these guys who fly the machines: their work's damned hard and dangerous and though they enjoy it it can't be often that they get a chance to do some straight fun flying. I guess that's what our pick up will be for them. Instead of hauling out broken bodies they should, touch wood, be taking off two successful climbers and with the spontaneous way they both offered I didn't have the heart to insist on being dogmatic about ethics. They very seldom make offers like that and would find a refusal hard to understand. What do you think?"

"I don't know really. I'm inclined to agree with you. At the start of the climb I'd have been categorically against it but after seeing the way these guys put themselves out for others I certainly wouldn't want to offend their feelings. But it's not one hundred per cent certain that they'll be able to pick us off, is it?"

"No, if there's a high summit wind then we're on our own but they'd probably be able to pick us up on the Italian side somewhere. Unless it storms we won't have to make the whole tedious way down to Entrèves. But I'm glad you can see the reasoning."

Happily unanimous, they went to sleep.

The night was long and cold but comfortable, they were ready to start at first light. The dark did not taper into any ominous in between shades and there were no warning signs in the deep blue of the 8 a.m. sky.

"A morning for climbing," laughed Jack, as he started on the first rope length.

There was one difficult swing over the chockstone and that was virtually it. The angle slanted; huge granite blocks, piled with snow but pregnant with holds, led up into the summit sunshine. It was all over. By 9.30 a.m. they were shaking hands, blinking behind dark glasses and looking down over acres of snow to the dark valley of Aosta in Italy. There was no great elation. They were still too wound up from concentration on the efforts on the wall. There was hardly any wind. Jack lazily muttered:

"Well John, that was a good one," and then, as if sealing their partnership, "What's next?"

"You're going to have to invite me on one of your expeditions."

"Might just do that."

An intrusion came slowly but insistently into their senses, changing their conversation.

"Well here it comes," shouted Jack pointing to the small dot of the Alouette over the Aiguilles. "I think he's going to be able to come in. If he does you go first: I'm more used to it than you."

"O.K."

Both sat watching expectantly, hardly allowing themselves to think that they could be down in Chamonix soon.

Bertrand was flying the Alouette, having tossed a coin with Cressier and won. He was accompanied only by Souchard his winchman, for the greater elevation of the summit made flying more difficult and their weight carrying potential less.

Gaining height slowly behind the Aiguilles du Géant, Bertrand brought them in along the crest of the Jorasses. Flicking his radio open he snapped: "They're on top. I'm going in."

Down in Chamonix, the Chief, Moncher, Maurice, the guides and half the Gendarmerie were crowded into the radio room listening. Flicking off the radio to aid his concentration, Bertrand flew slowly up the South side of the Pointe Walker.

"There's hardly any wind. I'm going right in," he shouted to Souchard.

They could see the two figures ducking to avoid the blast of powder that the rotors picked up from the summit. Slowly he manoeuvred into position until he was about ten metres above them. The wire snaked down. Jack clipped John into it and gave a thumbs up. Conditions were so good that Bertrand was able to hold it steady and in a few seconds John was sprawling in a mess of crampons and rucsacs on the floor of the machine looking up into Souchard's grinning face. Quickly he unclipped from the winch and crawled into a corner while Souchard sent it down again to Jack. In a few minutes he was clipped on, waving his thumb, and Bertrand took off down the North Side towards Chamonix with Jack still swinging free on his steel thread, peering down at the wall where he had spent one of the hardest weeks of his life. Then he too was sprawled in an unceremonious bundle on the floor, grinning widely and being grinned at in return.

Bertrand gave a laconic wave and switched on the radio. His voice boomed into the control room. "I have the cargo on board."

The room erupted into a spontaneous cheer.

In the chalet Walter, Steve and Susie were eagerly tearing into eggs and coffee when the phone rang. Walter answered and started dancing round the room with the receiver in his hand. "O.K. Maurice, fantastic." He put it down, beaming. "They're in the helicopter."

Susie dropped the frying pan with a crash, grabbed Steve and buried her head in him.

"Jesus, I can hardly believe it."

Walter continued mildly, "Yeah and they're bringing them straight round here so you'd better get back over that stove."

As the helicopter slowly settled on the pad John and Jack jumped out, feeling surrealistic with the sudden change and looking otherworldly to the watchers, their wind burned faces, deep sunken eyes and ripped, snow encrusted clothes. Slapping them on the back, people tried to shake their hands, talking all at once in a babble of French and English. Maurice hugged Jack, whispered the plan of campaign in his ear, and rushed them to the chalet to revive before the press conference scheduled for that afternoon.

The next two hours were occupied with the incredible luxurious delights of having a hot bath, each slowly feeling his way back to reality, and sitting down to platefuls of bacon and eggs washed down by coffee under Susie's watchful eye. She kept herself busy, avoiding Jack's eye until finally he grabbed her and sat her down on his knee. She promptly burst into tears.

"Well, Jesus, what's happening now?" laughed Jack.

Between sobs Susie eventually got out. "I'm so happy to see you both alive and here. For a time it seemed you'd be away for ever."

Further surprises awaited. Charlie and Judy had arrived about an hour earlier, having hired a car and driven the short distance from Geneva Airport. Dupré in his usual diplomatic but suspicious fashion had been friendly and polite but would not tell them where Jack and John were: he told them to wait until the press conference. But when he saw the welcome they gave John all his doubts were dispelled. John could not believe his eyes.

Charlie merely winked: "We thought you'd need some après climb comfort my boy," he flashed the inside of his jacket so that John could see a destructive bottle shape. "Thought you might need a dram."

John laughed and put his arm round Judy.

"I don't think I'll need much to put me to sleep but that'll certainly do it."

Soon they were introduced to the rest of the group as the press and television filed in, most in a somewhat disgruntled mood after being recalled from Italy, Megève Airport or hotels in Chamonix. It was a strenuous session for Jack and John but on the whole everyone seemed well disposed towards them. They were simply heroes. The only hostile one was Mureau of L'Echo, who seemed put out that he was not in control of the story on his own territory. It was he who asked the only real leading questions: "Why did you continue?" and "Why were you picked up from the top by helicopter?"

Jack took both questions and gave the standard answer to the first and a somewhat elusive answer to the second. "Well if Bertrand comes in waving a winch wire at you it would be very boorish not to accept a lift. Wouldn't you think so?"

Mureau did not answer, and they trooped outside to have pictures taken beside the helicopters with all those involved in the rescue.

When everyone had rushed off to file their stories the Chief's whisky started circulating and Charlie's bottle magically joined it.

Afternoon rolled on into evening and everyone eventually crammed into Maurice's apartment where his wife had put together a cold buffet. They were watching the news on television when Maurice came in clutching the evening edition of L'Echo, convulsed with laughter and handed it to Jack.

Somebody didn't like you after all," he pointed to the headlines of L'Echo.

"NEW ROUTE ON GRANDES JORASSES?"

"RESCUERS RESCUED BY HELICOPTER FROM THE SUMMIT."

Jack in turn burst out laughing, showing it to John.

"Oh well, you can't please everyone."

Dupré interrupted philosophically raising his glass. "The more brilliantly you succeed in this world the more enemies you get: the envious—those who would like to be in your shoes but can't. But my only advice as an old cynic is to ignore them and carry on. Here's to it." They all drank to the last semi-serious note of the evening. For once the two tired climbers were able to relax totally and forget about the mountains outside, content and happy in the friendly company: Charlie, catching up on the gossip with Maurice; Judy, eyes shining, realising that she was in deeper than she had thought; Walter and Steve, capable and lively, waiting for the next big one; Joan, teased by Lucien but watching Jack's arm round the giggling Susie; Barbara, tactful for once, and a host of others. But there was still this thing between them that separated them from the others, a depth of experience they could never hope to have understood. But next morning they would wake up and the mountains would still be there and their minds would slowly turn to thoughts of—the next one.

GLOSSARY

Bergschrund   The large crevasse that separates the steeper mountain face from the easier angled glacier slopes that accumulate below it. Bergschrunds usually mark the end of the approach and the beginning of the main climb.

Belay   A secure anchorage to rock or ice achieved by the use of pitons, the rope, nuts, slings etc. One climber is secured to the belay (belayed) while the other man climbs. They are linked by the rope which is paid out, or taken in, around the belayer's body or through a special friction belaying device (Figure of Eight, Sticht Plate etc.). In the event of a fall, providing rope and belay hold firm, the party is always secured to the mountain. Running belays, which work on a pulley principle, can be placed as the leader progresses to shorten the length of any possible fall.

Crampons   Steel frames fitted with spikes that are strapped to the soles of boots for climbing ice, snow and iced-glazed rock. Sharp protruding front points enable the climber to move quickly up steep ice slopes that would otherwise require step-cutting.

Figure of Eight   A metal device used to support the climber while he makes a controlled slide down a fixed rope (abseiling, rappelling etc.). It can also be used as a friction tool in belaying. The rope is passed around the implement in a special way to achieve increased friction. Further turns allow the rope to be locked in a fixed position. The principle is similar to that of a Capstan. Other friction devices are Sticht Belay Plates and Karabiner Brakes.

Jumars   A pair of mechanical devices that fit on the rope, slide easily up it but lock solid when downward force is applied. Footslings and waist loops are added to enable climbers to use jumars for steep prussicking (climbing fixed ropes) without undue exertion. The cammed locking teeth are prone to clogging with ice and grit that can lead to failure in support; because of this jumars are best used on clean, non-iced ropes. When bad conditions are inevitable Gibbs Ascenders or Hiebler Clamps can be used. These work on a different principle by bending the rope rather than biting it, but they are not as convenient to use as Jumars.

Karabiner   A strong metal snaplink that is used to link the rope to the climber, belays or running belays. A climbing team will usually carry between ten and forty karabiners depending on the scale and technicality of the climb. In the event of a fall karabiners may have to withstand great strains. Typical mountaineering karabiners are designed to withstand shock loads of between 2000kg and 5000kg.

Pitons Ice pitons, screws, rurps, bongs, knife-blades, angles, Leepers etc. All are metal nails and screws of various shapes and sizes that can be hammered or screwed into rock or ice to form secure belays or running belays. On a climb of the scale described in this book as many as thirty different pitons might be carried.

Tent Sac A small self-contained tent, without poles, that can be suspended from pitons to protect cramped bivouacs. It is made from strong lightweight, waterproof material and is usually wedged-shaped to match the shape required on a typical bivouac ledge. A sealed floor and zipped flaps enable the climber to gain a degree of protection in bad weather, but good technique is required to avoid serious condensation.

Terrordactyl A special type of ice axe with a short handle and a sharply inclined straight pick (reminiscent of the beak of the Pterodactyl). It is used for climbing very steep ice. The climber hammers his two Terrordactyls and his crampon points into the ice and gains height with their support. By these means his speed on difficult ground is greatly increased (compared to conventional technique using an ice axe and often involving step-cutting).